Drago's Touch

Inspirational Billionaire Romance

N R Emerald

Emerald Stone Publishing

Published by Emerald Stone Publishing

Print Book ISBN #: 978-976-97138-5-7

eBook ISBN #: 978-976-97138-4-0

Cover Design by Lynelle Caines of Lyn Elle Creative

Book Layout Using Atticus

Line edited by Librum Artis Editorial Services

Proofread by Suzanne Durant

DEDICATION

CUH, Thank You for Standing with Our Sister and Friend.

Content Warning

Drago's Touch includes themes of past trauma, which are gradually revealed as the story unfolds. The trauma occurred off-page and in the character's past.

Contents

Prologue	1
One	5
Two	10
Three	15
Four	20
Five	29
Six	32
Seven	37
Eight	42
Nine	46
Ten	49
Eleven	53
Twelve	57

Thirteen	61
Fourteen	64
Fifteen	69
Sixteen	73
Seventeen	78
Eighteen	82
Nineteen	86
Twenty	91
Twenty-One	94
Twenty-Two	99
Twenty-Three	105
Twenty-Four	109
Twenty-Five	113
Twenty-Six	117
Twenty-Seven	122
Twenty-Eight	126
Twenty-Nine	129
Thirty	133
Thirty-One	137
Thirty-Two	141
Thirty-Three	146
Thirty-Four	148

Thirty-Five 152
Thirty-Six 155
Thirty-Seven 157
Thirty-Eight 160
Thirty-Nine 163
Forty 166
Forty-One 170
Forty-Two 174
Forty-Three 177
Forty-Four 180
Forty-Five 184
Forty-Six 189
Forty-Seven 194
Forty-Eight 197
Forty-Nine 200
Fifty 205
Fifty-One 209
Fifty-Two 212
Fifty-Three 216
Fifty-Four 220
Fifty-Five 224
Fifty-Six 228

Fifty-Seven	233
Fifty-Eight	237
Fifty-Nine	242
Sixty	245
Sixty-One	249
Sixty-Two	256
Sixty-Three	260
Sixty-Four	263
Sixty-Five	266
Sixty-Six	268
Epilogue	274
Blurb	281

Prologue

Aimee

I spent yesterday bent over the toilet bowl, suffering from what must have been the most severe case of food poisoning in recorded history.

I racked my brain, trying to remember what I ate. Watermelon salad. Salmon with broccoli. Two single squares of dark chocolate. Maybe it was the salmon. Never eating salmon again.

Today, I'm curled up on the sofa, my stomach cramping like it went twelve rounds with a heavyweight boxer and came out on the losing end.

Sweat dotted my forehead. The temperature outside, according to the weather forecast, was a cool twelve degrees Celsius—a little warmer than a typical February day in Paris, but not so warm as to make me sweat like when I haul my groceries up those steep stairs. I chose the apartment because it provided outdoor space for my plants; the patio made this apartment worth the torturous daily workouts up and down those stairs.

Right now, I wish I had a roommate—someone to help me through this.

I'm alone. All this success...and alone. I longed for home. Home. Where was home? Etim or Sri Lasara. Not Sri Lasara, although I missed the beautiful waters of the Indian Ocean. Both Mom and Dad were gone now.

Dad gone. No more calls checking in on me.

Sri Lasara. No longer home. Nothing there.

Before I could wallow more in my misery, another punch to the stomach hit, this time accompanied by a warm gush between my legs. I was afraid to look, but I knew I had to.

Blood.

Thick.

Far from my usual cycle. Never had cramps like these before. If this was what my friends in high school complained about—not me, given my irregular cycle—they deserved my Miss World crown and some Olympic medals. Was this payback for all those missed periods?

I crawled off the sofa, leaving spots of blood behind me. Desperation fueled my movements as I grabbed my mobile and dialed Lazelle Parisienne, the fashion house with whom I'm under contract. When someone answered, I blurted, "Need an ambulance now!" There was no time for pleasantries.

Another punch—no, more like a kick—ricocheted through my body, and I dropped to the floor, sobbing. The pain was unbearable. Within five minutes, someone opened the door to my apartment and let the medics inside. The fashion house must have used their connections, thank goodness, as I was not in shape to make it to the door.

They found me curled up on the tile near the toilet bowl. Given my limited French and the gut-wrenching pain, when one medic leaned toward me, he sounded as if he were under water. I pieced together the words he said.

"Hang in there, we've got you."

Easy for him to say—he wasn't the one whose body was trying to kill him.

I must have passed out, because when I opened my eyes, the sterile smell of disinfectant filled my nostrils, and a voice echoed through the PA system. The sound bounced off the white tile walls, creating an eerie surround-sound effect. Turning my head, I focused on the person standing next to me. A pair of light blue eyes peered at me from behind glasses.

"Dr. Dolos, right?" I croaked.

She glanced up from her clipboard. "You're back again? Two months ago, you passed out from drinking too much. You really need to stay out of the ER." Her tone implied this was all my fault. Who in their right mind would want to make two trips to the ER in less than eight weeks, unless they were chronically ill?

"What's wrong?" I asked, my voice barely above a whisper.

"We did a CT scan. It's a hemorrhagic ovarian cyst."

"Dr. Dolos, I swear I'm not a heavy drinker. That night—"

"Look," she interrupted, cutting through my words with a sharp edge. "You can say whatever you want, but I've seen your records. You're not the first model to end up here." Her gaze bore into me, a mix of disdain and exasperation tightening her jaw. "I wish you'd leave the hospital for people who really need it."

She adjusted the drip with a swift, almost harsh motion, her frustration simmering just below the surface. The tension in the air thickened as she finished speaking. Her words stung more than I cared to admit. She shoved her hands deep into her coat pockets, her hard eyes lingering on me for a moment longer than necessary.

"I'll be back with your medication after I finish my rounds," she said, her tone clipped. "No surgery needed." Without another word, she turned on her heel, the sound of her footsteps echoing down the sterile hallway.

Either she hates me, or she has the worst bedside manner. Or both.

Despite what Dr. Dolos claimed, there was no way I drank that night until I blacked out.

No way.

One

Aimee

Five Years Later

She couldn't be serious!

Five years of torture. Therapy. The countless sleepless nights, struggling to fill in the blanks, for her to sit there and tell me I made this entire thing up? Was I truly losing my mind?

Penelope Jones came highly recommended by the chief of police as one of the best private investigators in Etim. I paid $20,000, believing she would get a breakthrough, and I would finally get some answers. Instead, she sat opposite me, the corners of her mouth pulled down, her shoulders hunched. Her eyes shifted, avoiding mine.

The café bustled around us, a jarring contrast to the stillness at our table. The constant clinking of dishes and hissing of the espresso machine mirrored the chaos in my mind. Once comforting, the rich aroma of coffee now left an acid taste in my mouth.

Tracing my finger around the rim of my now empty coffee cup, I said, "I don't understand."

Her brown eyes finally met mine. "Ms. Patel, everything I've heard about you makes you appear to be an upstanding citizen."

Where was she going with this conversation?

My eyes snapped to meet hers. "I don't understand what you're telling me."

"Let me repeat," she said, lowering her voice, as if she was speaking to a five-year-old child. Or like I was fragile, and she was afraid I would break. There was nothing left to break. But seeing my best friend, Topaz, face her demons and find happiness, I wanted the same for myself. If not happiness, then peace.

Peace.

I would settle for the peace of knowing what really happened.

Penelope continued. "I visited the hospital. A Dr. Dolos never worked there."

"I'm telling you, they're lying." My voice rose with agitation. "Twice. Not once, but twice, Dr. Dolos treated me."

A frown creased her forehead, and her eyes again moved away from mine.

"Ms. Jones, I'm not crazy," I insisted, my voice trembling. "I remember her perfectly. The look of disdain. Her blue eyes. That memory is sculpted in my mind."

A flash of five years ago crashed into my mind. The sterile hospital room, walls too white, too cold. The sharp sting of disinfectant in the air. Dr. Dolos looming over me, her lip curled into a sneer. Her gaze pinning me to the chair, shrinking me, crushing me under its weight, as if I were nothing, especially on the second visit.

"I'm not saying you are," Penelope said, pulling me back to the present. "I even asked a friend of mine to check the hospital records." She leaned forward and spoke in hushed tones. "I got them to hack into their system. There was never a Dr. Dolos working there."

Ms. Jones, with her braids pulled into a ponytail, exhaled as if she had been holding her breath for days, though we had been sitting in this café for less than twenty minutes.

She shook her head, and as she spoke, her next words floored me: "And there were no records of either of your visits."

My face burned, then went cold. My hands shook. I removed them from the coffee cup before it ended up on the floor.

Leaning forward, I responded, through clenched teeth, "I'm. Not. Making. This. Up."

Penelope Jones sat straighter in her chair. "The money you paid covered all expenses and costs. I don't want to take advantage of you or waste your time like some other PIs would do. Everything was a dead end."

"What are you saying?" I lifted my eyes, pleading, hoping I wasn't hearing what she was implying. I finally got the courage to look into what happened all those years ago, only to come up with nothing.

No—she found out something...that I was full-blown Crazy with a capital C. But I wasn't. Dr. Dolos existed.

Existed and appeared to hate me for existing. That much I was certain about.

"Ms. Patel."

"Aimee. Call me Aimee."

Reaching out her hands to cover mine, she said, "I'm sorry. I can't tell you to drop it and move on with your life. Or get help." Holding my eyes, she added, "Another kind of help, you know what I mean."

Pulling my hands away, I said, "Five years of therapy. Not one. Not two. Five years it took me to get to a point to go digging in my past."

Five years of my life on hold. All because of something—someone—that apparently never existed.

"Sorry," she offered, opening a leather folder she rested on the table when she first sat down. "You don't strike me as a person who is prepared to walk away." Pushing a card toward me, she said, "If there is anyone that can help you, it's that company. But their client list includes Fortune 100 companies and the super-rich elite. I'm not even certain they would see you. But they are your best bet."

I took the dark gray card and turned it over. It was embossed with the initials BI, an email address, and a contact number.

Standing, she offered, "Fortunately for you, they recently opened a base in Etim."

She left me staring at the small card in my hand, the weight of it far exceeding its size. Around me, the café continued its rhythm, oblivious to the fact that my world had shattered—again.

Two

Aimee

Topaz and I stepped into the elevator, which gleamed as if someone's sole job was to keep it spotless. My friend slipped her hand into mine and gave it a gentle squeeze. I hadn't asked if she believed me. She even asked her husband, Shae, to have Holly—who worked as part of his sister's security team—investigate. And Holly, I swore, could find anyone, even those buried in unknown graves. But she found nothing on Dr. Dolos. Even I wondered if I'd dreamed her up. Yet, Topaz never looked at me like I was crazy. She believed in me so much she got me into Baas International under the pretense of discussing cybersecurity for their new resort in Etim, set to open in six months.

Squeezing her hand, I mumbled, "Thank you."

"You rented an entire plane to bring me home. This is nothing. This is what friends do."

"You think they'll kick me out once they realize it's me?" I dropped my voice in case there were listening devices. With an elevator this clean, I was certain someone might be listening. *My gosh, I'm sounding paranoid.* I continued, "Will they be angry it's me and not the Anson Group wanting their services?"

Real estate was a thriving industry in Etim, with new buildings constantly popping up and old ones being torn down. I recalled looking for warehouse space last year and coming across this listing. I was certain it said the building had twenty-two floors and underground parking. But the lift buttons went from one to twenty. Maybe I got it wrong. That seems to be the recent thread running through my life at present. Studying the panel, another odd thing: there was no button with the number nineteen.

With a soft ding, the elevator stopped on the twentieth floor, and we exited. I pulled my head up, inhaling deeply in an attempt to absorb the confident energy pulsing from the charcoal gray walls. The receptionist sat behind a sleek, modern desk with the company's simple BI logo, its gold and silver foil catching the light and adding a touch of sophistication to the room. The air was crisp and clean, hinting at the professional atmosphere that filled the space.

Topaz stepped forward and smiled at the receptionist as he stood to greet us. "Good morning," she offered.

His intelligent eyes remained focused on her. His movements were precise, almost robotic. The sharpness in his gaze and the way he scanned the room made it clear he was more than a receptionist. The muscles straining against his tailored jacket hinted at readiness, as if he could neutralize a threat in an instant.

"Good day, Mrs. Anson and Ms. Patel. I'm Jaden." His strong, solid hand gave us firm handshakes.

How did he know our names? Topaz asked her administrative assistant to make the appointment, indicating that a representative of the Anson Group wished to meet with them, not specifying who would attend. Topaz, I understood. Since marrying Shae Anson, she's been featured in the newspaper more often than the editor-in-chief.

Did they use facial recognition technology between the elevator and here to identify us? I planted a smile on my face, hoping it projected confidence instead of worry. Last night's fears returned, twisting my stomach into knots. I almost felt ready to run right back to the elevator.

While Topaz handled the pleasantries, I wondered how I was going to get in to meet with them and convince them to take my case if they knew who we were by name. Deep in my bones, I believed this was my last hope of knowing the truth of what happened in Paris.

"Mrs. Anson, we will be ready to see you shortly. Have a seat, and I will come and escort you when the meeting is ready to begin." His dark, intelligent eyes connected with ours, assessing us like an android gathering information to report to the top brass. After offering cold or hot beverages and some cucumber and smoked salmon sandwiches—which Topaz accepted, but I refused—he left. Since Paris, I avoided salmon, especially with my stomach already in knots.

Maybe we didn't think through how this would work. All I wanted was ten minutes to plead my case. There was no price tag too big for my peace of mind. But knowing who we were, they might not allow me inside. Even though I'm a close friend, talking cybersecurity for a company that size is not something they would want to discuss in my presence. Even I knew they would consider it a security risk.

While Topaz calmly ate her sandwiches, my worry about getting inside to speak with those who would decide if they would take my case made my stomach churn. I'd stayed up late last night, watching gymnastics and worrying about today. The gymnasts' elegance and strength fascinated me. Instead of being interested in the competition, what caught my attention was the endurance and fearlessness displayed in performing those routines. The confidence. Yes, their confidence. For all those reasons, I watched. If I could muster a tenth of what they demonstrated, I could get through these next few minutes.

Five minutes later, he returned. His commanding presence was heightened by the perfect cut of his suit. Taking the tray, he had set for Topaz, he said, "I will return to take you."

Again, Topaz smiled and nodded, as though this was just another day and not a giant escalation of my worry. This was not going as planned. When he turned his back, I whispered, "They know our names! Our original plan of me going in instead of you will not work."

"Plan B."

Arching my brow and trying to keep my stomach from tumbling and flipping before I threw up from sheer stress, I whispered, "Plan B? There's a Plan B?"

"Now there is."

As Jaden approached us, Topaz turned and asked, "Aimee, can you help me?" Rubbing her stomach, she added, "Crap, I forgot about the morning sickness."

The young man paused, staying a respectful distance in the event that Topaz gave in to her morning sickness.

"In my first trimester. Morning sickness and feeling lightheaded at times is no fun," she said, smiling at Jaden.

Glancing at the two of us as I wrapped my arms around Topaz's shoulders in support, he commanded, "Follow me." Yes, it sounded more like a command or order.

As he pushed open the door, Topaz turned and asked him, "Nearest bathroom?" He motioned for her to follow him, and I slid into the door Jaden pushed open. My eyes connected with the sole person in the room.

The world tilted, and my legs turned to jelly, threatening to give way beneath me. My stomach didn't flip. It fell, hitting the floor hard.

"Holy crap!"

Three

Drago

Aimee Patel's eyes ping-ponged between me and the door. Her hand rested on the handle. Not about to ease her discomfort, I pointed to the dark gray high-back chair at the boardroom table. She edged toward the chair closest to the door. Keeping my hand pointed to the chair adjacent to me, I said, "This is a big room. No need for us to shout."

Opening her mouth and shutting it again, she reminded me of a puppet show I saw as a kid, but without the ventriloquist. She glanced at the door again and blurted, "I…need to check on Topaz."

"Ms. Patel, we both know Mrs. Anson isn't coming back anytime soon. Let's not waste my time."

She froze, her eyes widening as she realized the implication. Her grip on the door handle tightened, her arm tensed. "I knew it. I knew a place like this had to have cameras and listening devices," she said, her voice trembling but gaining a slight edge. "How dare you listen in on people's conversations!"

In my line of business, I've learned that people seldom tell the truth when they meet with you. They practice the polished, sanitized version they wish to present to me. As they wait, they finalize their story with their attorneys, colleagues, or friends. Sometimes, even to themselves.

"Are you ready to take a seat? We have ten minutes. I'll take two. You'll still be billed our consultation fee of $5,000."

"Ten minutes?" she asked, holding onto her bag strap.

I nodded in confirmation.

Aimee's eyes flickered with uncertainty, but there was a spark of determination. "If it is ten minutes, I get all ten minutes I'm paying for. You can talk after my time is up."

"My office. My business. My rules. You can leave now, but I will still invoice you for the time."

She hesitated for a moment, then squared her shoulders and strode to the seat opposite the one I pointed to. The initial fear in her eyes had been replaced with a simmering anger. I preferred an angry, seething Aimee Patel to a scared woman looking to dart out of my office.

I recalled meeting her when she and her best friend, business partner, and accomplice came to check on me under the guise of distributing New Year gift baskets, when I first moved to Etim. I had leased one of their villas after deciding to establish a base here. She was attractive—hell, gorgeous. But she didn't wear it like a badge or privilege.

Pulling out the chair and settling her handbag in the one next to her, she lifted her eyes to meet mine, wetting her lips. Her hands trembled slightly, but she steadied them, a sign of her growing resolve. Something tugged in my stomach. Since Minerva, I'd only attempted one relationship; it lasted a month and a half. She was more my type than Ms. Patel. An academic. Two years older than me. She had her act together.

Ms. Patel was so not my type. So, what the hell was that stirring? Purely a physical response to a beautiful woman.

"I'm sorry for the pretense," she said, lifting her eyes to study my face. Her voice was firmer now, the tremor mostly gone. "But you're my last option."

"How did you find out about this company? We don't advertise. We don't even have a website."

"My former PI, Penelope Jones. She gave me a card, said she didn't have the resources to continue the investigation, but maybe this company could help."

Penelope Jones was known for her unwavering integrity, a trait perhaps inherited from her family of law enforcement professionals. Given her impressive background in the police force, it was no surprise that she came highly recommended by them. Our technical operations head, Bishop, who also has a stake in the business, approached Ms. Jones with an offer to join our team. Her dismissal and passing the business card to Ms. Patel spoke volumes—she had no interest in joining us. It's a shame, as she would have undoubtedly been a valuable addition. But some people are content with their smaller operations.

Glancing at my watch, I said, "You have six minutes remaining."

She took out her mobile, set the timer for five minutes, and told me about Paris, Dr. Dolos, and all that Ms. Jones found. Or rather, not found.

When her alarm went off, she focused her eyes on me. "All I'm asking is for you to look into it. I want to put all this behind me and move on. I can't take a drink unless I see the bottle opened in front of me or mixed where I can see the bartender. I don't date because there are too many variables. I fly private to ensure I know exactly what I'm consuming. I can't continue like this... Living—actually, not living, existing—and barely so."

"Your eight minutes are up. Seeing that this meeting was arranged so I can discuss the Anson Group's new hotel in Etim, I expect your friend Topaz Anson to make good on her meeting. I'll also be billing them for this time."

"Are you crazy?"

"They called and booked." Leaning forward, I caught a whiff of a light floral scent. "We don't do PI work for individuals, unless you're super-rich, elite, or a head of state. Despite your wealth, good looks, and connections, you're what we call an 'average citizen.' We don't waste our valuable resources on average citizens."

Her head jerked up as if I shocked her.

I spread my hands out in a don't-blame-the-messenger gesture. "You don't fit our client profile."

"I would pay anything for you to look into it. Anything. Two weeks. One week. Even dedicate a day. Hours. Anything. I will pay."

I stood. "We're already over by fifty-eight seconds."

Ms. Patel remained seated and narrowed her eyes. "You said ten minutes."

"Correct. The remaining one minute and two seconds are to escort you to the door."

She stood slowly, her brow furrowing and her eyes darting between me and the door, as if trying to piece together what had just transpired. I strode toward the conference room door. "Don't forget your handbag."

Four

Aimee

Topaz told Mark, her driver—well, security, as he leads her security team—to take us to Tapas on the Bay. That much I heard. I rushed out of there so quickly Jaden didn't have an opportunity to escort us out. Topaz took one look at my face and followed me to the elevator. The logo was correct. BI—'Boastful Imbecile.'

"It was him," I stated flatly.

"Who?"

"Baas." One word defined him. Although it would be more apt without the "B" in front of it.

Topaz's eyes were trained on me, and I turned my head to gaze out the window. "What do you mean?" she asked.

Swallowing, I continued. "The renter from last year. The guy who rented our villa and turned up sixteen days after the fact. No wonder he didn't mix. Who mixes with average people when they don't breathe the same air? He didn't even give me a chance."

The passing scenery all merged as I fought not to hold onto the tears stinging my eyes. He was my last hope.

Topaz held my hand, her touch warm and reassuring. Did she think I was crazy and never wanted to tell me? The thought gnawed at me. She taught me to shoot. Although I owned a gun, I never carried it with me. I kept it in a secret compartment under my bedside table. She encouraged me to get therapy. Even when I decided to go digging, she never once said to leave the past in the past.

Turning to her, tears threatening to fall, I could see Tapas in the distance. I took a deep breath, my voice trembling. "Honestly. Do you think I'm crazy? That I made up this entire story because I can't face what happened? What I did?"

Topaz squeezed my hand tighter, her eyes never leaving mine. "Honestly, I wouldn't say either of us is exactly sane. Look at the crap we just pulled off. Wait until I tell Shae we need to meet with Baas International. But no, I believe you. Something happened, Aimee. We won't rest until we find out. Or, if you want to leave it alone, that's your call. But I believe you."

A tear slid out of the corner of my eye and down my cheek. I quickly wiped it away, trying to maintain some composure. "Let's drown my sorrows," I said, my voice steadier but still thick with sadness.

The young, smiling hostess greeted us with menus in hand and led us to a booth. The restaurant was alive with the chatter of diners, the clinking of glasses, and the occasional burst of laughter. The alluring scent of herbs and spices tickled my nose as I caught glimpses of decadent dishes passing by on trays. Across the room, a family celebrated a birthday, a small cake with a lit sparkler being presented as the group sang softly. None of it lifted my spirits.

Topaz mulled over the menu, but I already knew what I wanted. The server approached to take our order. Topaz ordered stir-fried chicken and shrimp on a bed of roasted vegetables. When the server turned to me, I said, "I'd like a cheeseburger with fries."

Topaz glanced at the menu, brows raised. The server's brows pinched together, and his lips pursed in thought. A restaurant of this nature did not serve cheeseburgers.

"Ms. Patel, I'm certain our chef would make an exception for you."

"Thank you," I replied, my voice grateful but tired.

When he was out of earshot, Topaz muttered, "Aren't you getting ready for your fashion show?"

Sipping my water, I nodded.

"A cheeseburger and fries don't exactly sound like fashion show prep, especially with a little more than a week to go."

"Thank Jesus that my line of clothing is for everyday women. I think everyday women eat cheeseburgers and not just salads all year round to fit into clothes. At least I hope not."

Topaz burst out laughing. "Aimee, despite all the crap we've been through, we can still laugh. You haven't lost your sense of humor."

I wished I could order a slice of cheesecake to go with the burger, and I don't even like cheesecake that much. Drowning your sorrows in food is bad, but right now, I didn't care. "I wish he had given me some hope that he would look into the Paris incident."

After sipping the water that was poured from the bottle opened at our table, I continued, "Not even thirty minutes could he spare. Not even that."

Drago

Jaden and I went over the report Bishop submitted on the Global Financial Consortium. If not for the farce of a meeting that was supposed to be with the Anson Group, this would have been completed. During my brief meeting with Ms. Patel, Jaden ran some analyses on the report about the Global Financial Consortium, known as GFC. They acted in the shadows, preying on developing countries that were unable to receive or seek funding from the World Bank or IMF. Their money came at a high cost, and they were often willing to blackmail heads of state, ministers, senators, whoever, to get what they wanted.

As sharp as Jaden's mind was, his body was lethal. I've worked with him in the field. Not yet thirty, Jaden could kill a man in more ways than I can count. When we decided to start the business four years ago, he was our first recruit.

After Aimee left, I pored over the GFC report, but her gray pleading eyes haunted me. I could not shake them. They were just as striking as when I first saw them up close, nearly a year ago. Mostly gray, but with a circle of near-black on the outer rim. Eyes slightly slanted.

It was a long day, not even counting the drama with Aimee Patel. Pushing open the door, entering the living room. Why was I even still thinking about Aimee Patel? She might not be a woman to binge drink now, but back then, who knew? Being new on the modeling circuit, young and trying to fit in, maybe she didn't know her limits. Or was even plain reckless. I'm not spending my time going down rabbit holes for a girl.

Walking in, Sebastian lifted his head, a soft purr rumbling from his chest. His eyes met mine for a fleeting moment before he closed them again, indifferent, as if I were part of the background. He stretched lazily, content in his own world. He was an almost-perfect companion. Low maintenance, minus the litter box.

One of the best decisions I'd made after purchasing this building was deciding to convert the top two floors into my personal living space. Yes, it saved on the commute, but in Etim that was not a headache. Right under our office floor were two penthouses, one where Jaden and his young wife lived, and the other belonged to Bishop, for when he visited.

The type of fieldwork we did was dangerous and paid well. Dangerous in itself was an understatement. Governments paid handsomely to keep the work we did off the books, but each time, your life was on the line. My plan was to get wealthy and retire from that job while I was still young enough to spend time helping Minerva build her private online business: helping women who simply needed a listening ear. She was a full-time tenured professor, but that business was her joy. However, she never did get the chance to do it, but I kept it funded. Even thought of exploring an arm which focused on men.

Sitting on the sofa, without even thinking, I turned on the middle screen. My wall carried three screens: one a TV, the other a camera feed from my office, and one a wireless screen for my laptop. I rolled the recording to my meeting with Aimee. When they booked, they were informed the meeting would be recorded. So no breach of privacy here.

She looked tormented.

Sebastian, with his thick black coat that formed into a gray and white ruff around his neck, ambled over to me and rested his head on my thigh and purred.

"Hey, boy." Stroking his stomach, I gently admonished him. "Stacey fed you before I arrived. No fooling me." While stroking the arch of his back, my thoughts drifted to Aimee Patel. *Why can't I get her out of my mind?*

She possessed a desperation I've not seen for a while. Almost like a drug addict looking to score a fix.

My mobile rang. Glancing at the number, my brows furrowed as I answered. "Luna, something wrong?"

"Can't your sister-in-law call you?"

Minerva and Luna were sisters, but in personality and appearance, they were nothing alike. Luna, older by six years, more resembled their mother, with a fair complexion and copper-gold hair. Minerva had a tanned complexion and long curly hair, taking after her Italian father, who her mother married after her first marriage ended in divorce.

"Luna, the last time you called me I had to bail you out of jail."

"Well, you can't blame me for throwing a brick into my cheating husband's car."

Resting my head on the back of the sofa, I refrained from telling her she should stop getting married. I've lost count. Was she on husband five or six?

Taking a deep breath, I asked, "What trouble have you gotten yourself into now?"

Luna laughed, her voice slightly slurred. "Nothing like that. Winter is getting married, and she wants you to give her away."

"Why didn't Winter call herself?"

"She's heartbroken. Her father is too busy to attend the wedding. I told her to ask you, but she said you wouldn't come because you've moved so far away."

I hoped Winter wasn't making the mistake of following her mother's poor example. Luna's view of marriage was like serial dating. With a thousand questions swirling in my head, I asked, "Who's this guy? I need details."

"No, you're not digging into him. He's a nice boy." She laughed. "They met at church. Something the two of us know nothing about. Winter is still holding out hope for me. She's such a sweet and innocent child."

"Is she still planning on going to university?"

"Yes, he will support her dreams."

"When is the wedding?"

Luna, in her singsong voice said, "They want a destination wedding. With her going to university and all. Two weeks. Wedding in two weeks."

"Two weeks." I'm in the middle of this GFC investigation. Maybe by then we would have decided whether to take the case.

"Um. Two. Two weeks."

Placing my phone on speaker, I demanded, "Where?"

"The Caribbean."

"The Caribbean?"

She purred, not sounding even half as alert as Sebastian. "You know...like Barbados, Antigua, Tobago. Cari—"

"I know where the Caribbean is, but why? And why so fast?"

"Destination weddings are all the craze. Plus, her father is footing the bill," she said with a bitter laugh.

"Luna, is this what Winter wants, or did you suggest this to her?"

"Joanna's divorced now. You can bring her as a date, or I can set you up with one of my friends. But you gotta have a plus one."

No way in hell am I taking my wife's best friend to a wedding. "Luna, I don't need a date."

"Yes, you do."

Pinching the bridge of my nose, I demanded, "Why?"

"Silly, it's being held at a couples-only resort. An Anson property. Actually, it is a private island owned by the Anson Group. Didn't you hear the part where I said her father is paying for the wedding? Only the best for my baby."

The name Anson jerked my attention back to the woman on the screen.

"Want Joanna's number? Can't disappoint Winter."

With my eyes focused on the woman on the screen, I muttered one word. "No."

Five

Aimee

Resting my cosmetic bag in the suitcase, I sighed. I preferred to travel light, but it wasn't possible this time. I closed the suitcase and glanced over at Topaz, who had an unreadable expression on her face. It appeared she didn't know whether to be smiling or frowning.

"It's finally here," I said, trying to sound excited. Sitting on the bed next to her, I added, "All the planning for this launch and online store. I can't even think about opening the store in London. That will be phase two. But I already have orders from stores."

"I'm going to miss it all," she mumbled.

I gave her a sympathetic smile. "If you get within five miles of an airport, Shae Anson will know. I agree with him. You had terrible morning sickness last week. The doctor even thought of hospitalizing you."

Sulkily, she replied, "I know." Perking up, she said, "You know I'll be praying. I know you've got this."

"Thanks." I paused, feeling a wave of anxiety. "While I'm out, there will be some small deliveries. Ask Mark to put them inside for me."

"That was a wise decision, to turn the duplex into your home office when we moved into our home," she said, trying to lighten the mood.

"It's a plus. Nothing beats our morning breakfast meetings. But life changes. I think even my orchids missed you lurking in the background, glaring at them. One even died, despite my efforts at resuscitation."

I slipped my hand around hers, squeezing gently. "Take care of yourself and my little niece or nephew."

Hearing the buzz of my mobile, it was probably the chopper alerting me they were on their way. As I grabbed the phone, my brows shot up. Unknown number. Maybe the call had to do with the upcoming show. Topaz, not missing a beat, saw the puzzled look on my face.

"What's up?" she asked, her curiosity piqued.

I held up a finger. "Hello?"

A deep, baritone voice greeted me from the other end. I snapped, "I'm not even going to ask how you got my number."

"Let's put it this way; if you wanted to hire my company, and I couldn't even track down a seven-digit number, then I should refund you your $5,000."

Returning to sit at the edge of the bed, I asked, "Decided to take the case?"

"Can you stop by on your way to the airport?"

I rolled my eyes, a mixture of annoyance and curiosity filling me. "So, you know, it's creepy that you know my flight plans, no matter who you are."

"Ms. Patel," he said, his tone clipped. "I have a proposition for you. Either you're interested or not."

Six

Drago

Jaden opened the door, and Aimee stepped inside. Our eyes connected. A stirring in my lower parts caught me off guard. It better stand down before I embarrass myself. Tight-fitting jeans, dark brown knee-length boots, and an off-white cashmere sweater wrapped around the waist of her jeans. Those long legs, I wonder—

I shook my head. Where did those thoughts come from? Lack of sleep, maybe. Given what I wanted to discuss, the last thing I needed was for her to think I was some sort of desperate pervert.

She stood by the door, as though some force field stopped her from venturing further into the room. Leaning against the closed door, she asked, "What's the proposition?"

There was a long side table with coffee, tea, and an array of fresh fruit. Maybe I should offer her something that might get her to venture further into the room.

Locking eyes with hers, I asked, "Are you always so eager?"

Something flashed across her face. It was almost as if I had slapped her. The average person would have missed it. Given my master's degree in psychology and years of training and fieldwork as an operative, I never missed much. Her reaction reminded me of the delicate balance I had to maintain in this conversation.

"You might have all day, but I need to be in London in the next few hours."

I took a deep breath, trying to steady my thoughts. This was not how I wanted to do this, but there was no going back now. "My niece—actually, my wife's niece—is getting married."

Aimee stood straighter, her eyes widening slightly. "You're married?" Shaking her head, she continued, "Your wife's niece is getting married. Why does that warrant me stopping before going to the airport?"

Her disbelief was so intense it seemed to fill the space between us, hanging heavily in the air. Despite the pang of sadness that came with mentioning my late wife, I pushed it aside and continued. "I want you to accompany me to the wedding."

Her hands flew to her hips. "Is this some sick joke? You want me to accompany you to your wife's niece's wedding?"

A crease formed between her brows. She was getting agitated. I could see the confusion and frustration building up. This was harder than I anticipated.

"Why can't your wife accompany you?" she demanded in a pitch several octaves above her usual.

Understanding flooded me. "She's dead."

"Who's dead?" she asked, eyes wide.

"I came about this all wrong. Please, sit." I needed to regain control of this conversation.

Sitting where she had last time, I turned my body toward her. "I really bungled this whole thing." Memories of my wife's ability to charm anyone flooded my mind.

Shaking my head, I clarified, "My wife is dead."

"Sor—"

"Please don't. I need a plus-one for the wedding, or Luna might find me a date from hell." The thought of Luna's attempts at matchmaking sent a shiver down my spine. For sure, I couldn't handle one of her setups.

She frowned, still processing. "I'm certain you have a list of women you can call."

Pinching the bridge of my nose, I tried to keep my patience. "Here is what I propose. For three days of your time, I will look into your matter and give you a fifty percent discount. Three days of work for $100,000."

Aimee arched her brow, her skepticism clear. "Where and when is this wedding?"

"Next weekend at a private island in the Caribbean. An Anson property. A couples' resort." I could see the suspicion in her eyes, and I couldn't blame her. The situation was absurd.

"Are you kidding me?"

"Do I look like the type that jokes?" My tone was more serious than I intended.

"Maybe you should try it sometime."

I couldn't help but smirk at her retort. "Three days."

She took a deep breath, leaning forward, as if considering my offer.

I did quick math and corrected myself. "Actually, it is four days. I have to be there next Thursday for dinner."

She settled back into the chair, absently drawing her long hair over one shoulder. I blinked, suddenly aware of how my gaze followed the movement. The casual gesture shouldn't have been distracting, yet here I was struggling to remember my next sentence. When did hair become sexy? Maybe this entire thing was a bad idea. Well, obviously it was a very bad idea. But I couldn't back out now.

"Four days. Stay in the same room as you?"

"Suite. I will get a suite."

"A two-bedroom suite." Leaning forward, she said, "Your offer is a little weak on benefits. Four days, same room, travel from the Mediterranean to the Caribbean, literally halfway around the world and charging me $100,000 for the privilege?" Resting her hands on the table, she countered with her own offer. "One week of investigating my matter for $100,000."

Studying her, I said, "If after the week I tell you there is nothing?"

Her shoulders slumped. The doubt and resignation in her eyes were clear. I wanted her to move on. It's amazing how often people cannot accept and even believe their mistakes.

"Would I have to act like we're a couple? Touching and holding hands?"

"This isn't some romantic comedy. We're not fake dating. I'm happily single."

She stood and tilted her head down toward me as I remained seated. "Who's Luna? And why me?"

Rocking back in my chair and locking eyes with her, I admitted, "Luna is my sister-in-law." Exhaling, "I wish I could say it's because of your striking beauty and charm. But honestly, you're desperate." Her brows shot up, almost flying off her face.

"You're desperate for help with this case. And I want uncomplicated."

Seven

Aimee

Since shaking Drago's hand yesterday and saying, "Deal," I'd been certain I could ask Topaz to get Drago's need for a plus-one waived. But I don't want to abuse our friendship. They're already meeting with him next week. Shae laughed and agreed to the meeting when she confessed. Although Topaz will be the one running the Etim resort, Shae makes all major decisions for security for any arm of their businesses.

No, I can do four days. Thinking about the fact that he would be the first man I've been alone with since waking up in that hotel room years ago, not knowing how I got there... *No, Aimee. Focus.* In less than two hours, I will hit the runway, answering the question every fashion magazine and news outlet has been wondering—was I was returning to modeling?

For my show? Hell, yes.

Drago, the wedding, and everything that came with it could wait until tomorrow. No, it could wait until next week. That trip would determine if the hundreds of thousands of dollars I've spent sitting in Dr. Taitt's office had paid off.

Holly walked in, followed by a team of stylists. Holly, with her sharp eyes and poised demeanor, agreed to oversee security for this event, given it was being held at the Anson's hotel in Mayfair. "Aimee, everything is in place," she said, her tone steady and reassuring.

Her words signaled that it was time to push all thoughts of Drago out of my mind and focus on the business of launching Blue Orchid. *Clothing Designed to Make Every Woman Feel Like a Queen*.

There was a buzz backstage. Glancing around the room, I realized it reminded me of Etim. All shades and sizes of women, with not one of them ever having set foot on a runway before. I hand-selected each of the thirty women. Last month, all the women came and overnighted at this hotel. Partly for preparation, but more importantly, I wanted them to bond. Some were mothers, glad for the night off. Nurses and administrative assistants, who were happy for the break. The oldest lady was a grandmother of three, who claimed to be sixty-five on her application, but the woman looked not a day over forty. The only thing that made me believe her was the silver in her hair, because there was not one line on her beautiful dark skin.

So many things could go wrong. Thank God for Topaz's prayers.

Each woman had two changes, including me. There were three segments: Office to After Work, Cocktail to Formal, and Blue Orchid Intimates.

When I hit the runway to end the formal wear section, I would silence all the speculations about my return.

Laney, the show director, called out, "Ten minutes to show time!" She moved through the room at a brisk pace, her iPad held tightly to her chest.

Taking deep breaths, I offered up a quiet prayer. "Lord, I know I only call on you in desperate times. Please let all go well in spite of my fickle ways." With that, I ran my shaking hands through my hair, arranged my face into a confident smile, and called the women over to gather around me.

I studied each one of their faces. "Let's show the world we got this!" I said, trying to keep my voice steady.

The Office to After Work segment came off without a hitch. Those ladies were changing, and the end of the Cocktail to Formal segment was approaching. I was wrapping up this section wearing a dark blue halter gown with a ballroom skirt. The dress looked so innocent at first glance, but with my hair over my shoulder, it hid what was keeping the dress up. The dress showed off the bare skin on my back all the way to my waist. When I hit the runway, the flashes popped like fireworks, the dark blue effect of the lights gave me a peek at the high tables scattered around the room, each featuring a pot of orchids. The attendees could see me, but it was hard to see them. That also made it perfect for the ladies. It reduced their nerves.

When I turned, I paused and glanced over my shoulder, so they could get the full effect of the dress.

This work could really give you an adrenaline rush. Either you loved all those eyes on you for the thirty seconds, or it was just another job. This time, it was a mixture. This was my hard work. I wanted them to love every piece. I normally would stride off, but deciding to be a little playful, I stopped and gave a backward glance before leaving the runway and moving my hair from over my right shoulder to fall and cover my back. I wore my hair four inches longer than usual, with this show in mind.

Once back behind the curtain, I rushed to my dressing room. The intimate section was about to begin, and I was wearing the final piece of the night. No one had seen this piece, and I wanted this finale to be a showstopper. I hoped to pull it off. While the pieces were of varying colors, the ones I wore stuck to the Blue Orchid color theme.

Laney came over. “You’re on in two minutes. As you walk, we will roll the love seat out, as requested.” She gave me a reassuring pat on the shoulder, her eyes reflecting the same excitement that coursed through my body.

Stepping out again, I kept the long, blue silk robe tied. When I reached the end of the catwalk, I untied it, but did not reveal what was underneath until I returned to the love seat. Shrugging the robe off my shoulders with a shimmy, I revealed a blue, off-the-shoulder lace corset top and the matching, close-fitting cheeky bottoms. As I lay on the couch, my hair fell over the back, leaving me and my intimate wear fully exposed. At Laney’s cue, all the models returned in their last outfits, which gave cover to remove the chair. As the people stood and applauded, the models created an aisle with their bodies for me to walk through. I turned, my back to the audience, and they followed me off backstage.

When the final model had slipped behind the curtain, I threw my hands in the air and shouted, "We did it!"

Eight

Drago

It took less than two minutes to hack into Anson's cameras. I didn't know which would peeve Shae Anson more: if he found out that I hacked in or the fact that the system, although good, was easily penetrable by a professional hacker. From what little I knew about the man, both. Maybe I would keep this to myself.

Why was I doing this again? I'd never even picked up a fashion magazine. I had a stylist who visited twice a year and changed everything from casual clothes to tuxedos as he saw fit. Jaden arranged our tactical gear. If my clothes fit and were comfortable, I was good.

How long does a fashion show last?

When I gave up the struggle of debating whether to do this, the Cocktail to Formal Wear segment was starting. This was routine surveillance, I assured myself. She's my client. This was all research. I must say, the idea of not using professional models was brilliant. A curvy lady strutted down the runway in a knee-length, white, off-the-shoulder dress. An older lady followed her, wearing a flowing red pantsuit that complemented her dark skin. Anson's cameras were top-notch quality; this was like having a front-row seat. Better. I believe I could see more from right here on my living room sofa than those in the front row.

When people thought the last model had finished, she appeared. The buzzing. Lights flashing. My mouth went dry. Breathtaking. The blue gown revealed some of her shoulder, but when she turned, it exposed all that smooth skin. I believe I forgot to swallow. The mechanics of how my throat worked evaporated from my memory. She turned and stared, as if looking right at me. Her back, which was once bare, disappeared with a flick of her hand, her long black hair becoming a veil covering her exposed back. My fingers twitched, imagining the sensation of running them through her hair, or seeing it spread out against my gray bed—

Seriously, where are these thoughts coming from? Client. My interest here is the fact that she's a client.

The ladies returned with everything from comfortable pajamas to shorts and everything in between. Cotton, satin, and silk. The Blue Orchid Intimates were all about sleepwear. Smart woman—she structured the show from work to sleep.

An alert sounded, interrupting my trance. I glanced at the screen and spotted a new connection in the feed. Someone had joined the stream, rerouting it straight from Anson's cameras. My fingers moved quickly, pulling up the details. The digital trail led back to Etim. I shook my head, a wry smile tugging at the corners of my mouth. Of course, it was Topaz. I could almost see her now, grinning at her screen, pleased with herself for taking the roundabout route.

Aimee appeared again, this time in a long blue robe. Every gaze in the room was fixed on her. When she reached the end of the runway, she untied the belt holding the robe closed. Although untied, we remained in suspense. Like everyone else, I wanted to see what was under there. Then I saw the chair. She approached the chair and let the robe fall to the floor. My pulse quickened. All the blood from every part of my body went in one direction, and it throbbed as it rested against the zipper of my pants.

When she laid on the couch, I almost embarrassed myself. I was harder than iron. Glancing down at my self-imposed situation, I willed it to return to a normal state, taking in deep breaths to calm myself. I was grateful and disappointed when the ladies flooded back onto the stage.

As she came down the center, with the robe tied again, my eyes remained glued to the screen. The years of discipline and self-control seemed to be tied up like the robe that clung to her skin. I wanted to be clinging to her skin, too.

My mind screamed at me as my eyes remained fixed on the screen. *This deal was going to blow up in my face.* Turning off the laptop, I got up from the sofa and paced as I considered my options.

Sebastian lifted his head in my direction before re-curling himself back into a ball.

I strategize.

I calculate.

I don't make mistakes.

Mistakes are costly.

Aimee Patel may be my first mistake.

Nine

Aimee

After the show, I slept like someone who had fallen into a coma. When I awoke the following morning, I stepped into the living area of the suite. The day was overcast, so the light was on in the room. My eyes tugged toward a beautiful blue orchid in a stunning pot. The pot, crafted from fine porcelain, featured an intricate blue and white design reminiscent of ancient Chinese pottery. The pot featured yellow and white tulips along with flowing vines, which contrasted beautifully against the rich cobalt blue and the pristine white background. It was a work of art, yet it did not overshadow the magnificent orchid. My breath caught at its beauty, a small smile playing on my lips.

"That arrived an hour ago," Holly said, breaking the silence.

Turning to her, I replied, "It's beautiful. Was there a card?" My heart beat a little faster, curious about who had sent such a thoughtful gift. Before I could finish my sentence, the phone in the suite rang, and I answered.

"The show was fantastic! You know, for my birthday, I want one of those corsets." Topaz's voice came through the phone, bubbling with excitement.

I chuckled, warmth spreading through me at her enthusiasm. "I'm certain Shae likes you with nothing on," I teased.

"A girl needs to spice things up now and then," she responded with a laugh.

Laughing with her, "I'm not even going to ask how you saw the show."

"I hope you love my gift," she said, her tone softening.

I glanced at the orchid, and gratitude washed over me. "You didn't have to, but I absolutely love it." My voice was sincere, hoping she could hear the appreciation in it.

"But I wanted to," she insisted.

After ending the call with Topaz, I admired the orchid again. Its beauty tugged a smile from my lips. Checking the clock, I had sufficient time to get ready for the buffet breakfast I arranged for everyone who was a part of the show. I showered and changed into a long, blue, flowing linen dress with a broad, brown leather belt.

The breakfast room buzzed with excitement. The elaborate spread, suitable for a royal wedding, took center stage. Platters of fresh fruit, an assortment of pastries, and steaming trays filled with food created a feast to fill our starving stomachs. Or at least mine. There was no way I was eating before the show, and then the adrenaline rush made me too excited to eat after.

Animated conversations filled the air. "I'm getting a facial," someone said nearby. Sylvia, a registered nurse, added, "I'm getting a pedicure; I'm always on my feet." Their voices were laced with joy, and I wondered what the source of the excitement was, as it seemed to be more than just the buffet.

Curious, I strolled over to Laney, who was already gathering her breakfast from the buffet. "What are the ladies on about?"

"Everyone received a complimentary spa treatment from the hotel," Laney explained, her eyes twinkling with delight.

Trust Topaz to go over the top. Tears welled up in my eyes, and I quickly blinked them away, not wanting to draw attention. Every person deserved to have a friend like her in their corner.

Laney lifted her eyes to meet mine. "What are you having?" she asked, a knowing smile playing on her lips.

"I'll eat after everyone," I replied, my voice a bit choked with emotion.

"No," Laney insisted. "What are you having done at the spa so I can make you a booking?"

Shaking my head, I said, "Topaz already sent me my gift."

"Well, you're on the list," she argued.

Still shaking my head and observing everyone eating, I picked up a plate. Smiling, I thought, *Shae will not even know what hit him*. The corset nightwear comes with all bottoms, including a thong. I'm sending her a set in every color.

Ten

Drago

Long flowing hair.

Black.

Blacker than polished onyx.

Shaking my head. Snap out of it. Watching that show was a bad idea. No… a very, very bad idea. Since my wife's death, I tried a relationship once. On paper, the lady ticked all the boxes. But she aroused nothing in me, not even a spark. After a few weeks, we decided to be friends.

My dreams last night were X-rated. When I woke up, I couldn't decide whether to be disappointed they were dreams—or relieved. Even that bothered me. Lust. Plain and simple. I wasn't some wet-behind-the-ears young man.

I needed to lose these thoughts and focus. Minerva's loss was ever present. The ache and absence had lessened with time.

This distraction with Aimee was a layer of complication I didn't need.

Although I could imagine what happened five years ago, I would look into the matter and prepare a report so she could move on with her life. She would be returning to Etim tomorrow, and we would travel the following day to the Caribbean. Hopefully, I would have compiled the report for us to discuss. I would share the information on our return leg of the trip in an effort to allow her to have an enjoyable time. But why did I care about her feelings? When did that start?

Aimee Patel was a job. We were doing each other a favor. Nothing more.

Even if she did not like the findings, it would give her closure and allow her to move on with her life. Plus, it would remove this temptation from me.

The door pushed open, and Jaden entered and sat next to me at the conference room table. "Finished the report? Bishop is ready for the conference call."

"Ready." Pushing thoughts of Aimee aside, I focused on the matter at hand.

Bishop appeared on the screen, larger than life. The eighty-inch screen was installed into the wall in the conference room—and yes, sometimes we gathered in here and watched a game. His eyes zoomed in on me. "This is your call, Drago."

Both Jaden's and Bishop's eyes mirrored the weight and the importance of this decision. This was not one we ever take lightly.

"Having read the intel Jaden gathered on this GFC member, I'd do this for free. This guy is making deals to fund projects in developing countries to have an unlimited supply of organ donors."

Bishop's face twisted in disgust. "This is heinous. If we weren't risking our team's lives to bring this man down, I'd say to hell with the money."

Turning to Jaden, I said, "You're going in. The GFC wants to make it look like a natural cause. They'll put a new contact in place for that region."

"What he's doing to children and young adults, he deserves to suffer, not go quietly in his sleep."

I raised a brow at Jaden. "Seems like you've got a plan worked out."

Jaden leaned forward, his dark eyes locking on mine. "I knew we'd take this case. Not for the $100 million they're paying but for the moral and ethical principle."

We talked strategy for the next forty-five minutes. Based on the GFC member's schedule, he was planning a one-week holiday on his yacht in Greece.

"How much money do these people need? He's seventy-six and worth over two billion dollars and still wants more," Jaden said with a huff, buttoning his jacket.

"Money, no. For someone like him, this is about power. The feeling of playing God."

Bishop nodded. "Totally agree with you on the profile you've painted."

The meeting ended, and I turned to my coworker and friend. "Jaden, I know you'll be careful."

"Always," he responded. Reaching the door, he paused. "You didn't mention our other client..."

Raising a brow at him, I asked, "Other client?"

"I must be wrong. Maybe you're actually going on a date to an exotic Caribbean island with Aimee Patel." Whistling, he closed the door.

With the briefing meeting over, it was time to start my research. The easiest place, which should not be, was to search the hospital records.

After two hours, I found...

No Dr. Dolos.

No hospital records.

No lease.

After a fire, the owner, who was now deceased, sold the place where she lived, which someone transformed into a bed-and-breakfast. The modeling agency that signed her was no longer owned by the same person. Except for pictures of her on the Parisian runway, it was as if Aimee Patel never lived there.

Eleven

Aimee

Yesterday, I unpacked and repacked. Nothing short of a category six hurricane was going to stop me from keeping my arrangement with Drago. Based on my research, I learned that hurricanes went as far as category five.

Although I had not heard from Drago, I trusted him. Maybe it was the firm handshake, the steadiness of his eyes, or his no-nonsense attitude. All these factors made me trust him. In less than two hours, my suitcase was beside the door and ready for tomorrow. Given that I would be gone for four days, I had emails to respond to and a conference call that had to be done, so I could travel with a greater peace of mind.

In the lead-up phase to the launch of the Blue Orchid line, I used a virtual assistant service. But with the business now fully launched, the villas and the Blue Lightning Café— which are jointly owned by Topaz and me—required more attention.

With Topaz getting more involved with Anson Resort as it neared completion, she convinced me I needed a part-time assistant, someone to work at least two or three days a week, at least during the launch period. She was so right.

Many candidates applied, but most lacked the necessary experience. The poor quality of applicants caught me off guard. Then I met Leila. She recently graduated from university, and while she didn't have much experience, something about her resonated with me. Her passion for fashion, especially accessories, shone through in the interview. She brought her portfolio and showed me some pieces she had designed. Despite using semi-precious stones, her jewelry radiated elegance. Her enthusiasm and creativity mirrored my own when I first started, and that connection made my decision clear.

When I logged on, Leila was already waiting. Her green eyes twinkled with excitement as she said, "Ms. Patel, the orders are going to crash the website, especially for that lingerie showstopper you wore. I believe women are buying those things as if they were on sale."

"Aimee. Not Ms. Patel."

"Aimee," she echoed, testing it to see how it sounded coming from her lips.

Smiling at her, I nodded. "Let's hope our web manager ensures our website remains up. The stores in London will not get their merchandise until next week."

Kim, our website designer and manager, logged on and assured us there would be no problems. The E-commerce was working smoothly, and the orders were reaching our warehouses in London and Etim to ensure shipment. When Kim left the call, I said, "Thank you. I know the next few days will be hectic."

She waved a dismissive hand. "I should thank you!"

"I'm traveling tomorrow but call me if there are any problems."

"It's four days. You deserve a break after the last few days."

Before arming the house, I took a picture of the orchid Topaz sent. The pot was probably worth more than the marble side table where I placed it. My phone buzzed with a message from Drago:

> Black Range Rover BI7 will be waiting for you. It will be driven by Jaden.

Putting my suitcase in the trunk, I was thankful that he was sending Jaden. I would have booked my regular driver to pick me up, but Drago said he was making all the plans. His attention to detail and the way he took charge were both reassuring and unnerving. I trusted him, yet our arrangement kept my nerves on edge. Four days with a man I hardly know. I don't dare let my mind drift to the sleeping arrangements. Why didn't I get Topaz to ask Shae for the property to bend their rules on this occasion? Then I would not have to travel with Drago. He would have attended and not required a plus one.

Friends don't abuse friendship privileges. That's why you did not ask.

Lord, I hope that when this is all over, I will have some semblance of a normal life. Ride in a taxi. Call an Uber. Maybe not ready for the Uber yet, but one step at a time.

Twelve

Drago

I tracked the vehicle's movements to the office and pushed the door as Jaden pulled up. Jaden hopped out of the Range Rover, already checking his watch. I knew he was already mentally getting into mission mode. Slipping behind the wheel, the leather interior of the Range Rover exuded a faint, familiar scent mixed with the crisp morning air that had seeped in as we made our way toward the private airport in Etim City.

After boarding the plane, I focused on settling Aimee before studying the plans we already put in motion to remove the GFC member. After reviewing them, I placed my phone on airplane mode. I really did not need to go over those plans again, and I hadn't expected her to sit next to me when there were at least twelve other seats she could have chosen. Her powdery, sweet scent drove me to scan my phone for anything else to keep my mind occupied. The next eight hours would be torture. Why did this seem like a good idea two weeks ago?

Not being able to ignore her any longer, I asked, "Are you okay?"

"I should ask you. You appear a little tense. Do you need me to hold your hand during takeoff?"

I grinned. I might want her to hold my hand, but not for the reason she thinks. "I guess your smart mouth tells me you're good. After we check in, there is a dinner tonight. My wife's family can be a bit much. You don't have to attend, if you don't wish to."

Before returning to the tablet, which rested on her lap, she lifted a brow at me. "If they're going to give you a hard time, I wouldn't miss it for anything."

"Never saw you as sadistic."

Smiling, she replied, "I'm not. Just want to be there to see what ruffles the great Drago Baas."

Since Minerva's death, I have always gone solo to any family events. Despite her passing, they still view me as family. Glancing at Aimee out of the corner of my eye, I was certain they would love her, especially Winter.

She looked stunning in green- close-fitting pants and a cream-colored, off-the-shoulder top, complemented by a nude bag and shoes. As the plane leveled out, I was glad to see the flight attendant approaching. I needed a distraction.

"Can we have two sealed bottles of water with lemon? We will open and pour the water ourselves."

Aimee's shoulders relaxed slightly after she heard my request. She leaned into me, bringing all her sweetness into my space, assaulting my nose, and whispering, "Thank you."

"On this trip, know you're safe with me."

Her gray eyes held mine without blinking. "I know."

Those two words settled in the pit of my stomach, stirring something deep inside. They chipped away at the barriers I'd built around me since Minerva's death. At first, I believed Aimee was wasting my time. She'd gotten drunk and couldn't remember what she did next. She was young and had a reckless moment. But now, I wasn't so convinced.

Touching her hand and not wanting to bring up anything about my investigation yet, I said, "I want you to know, I will get to the bottom of what happened to you five years ago."

"Have you—"

"When I have something concrete to report, I will tell you. But yes, I've started."

She grabbed my hands, and tingles rushed all over my body. Eyes glistening with tears, she mouthed, "Thank you."

The flight attendant brought water, along with an assortment of nuts and dried fruits for us to share. The subtle rustle of the snack packets and the clink of the bottles provided a brief respite from the tension.

Aimee went back to reading, and I pulled out my laptop. Two hours into the flight, the windows dimmed, casting a calming twilight over the cabin. Aimee turned off her tablet and got comfortable. Thirty minutes later, while I concentrated on a report, Aimee's head landed on my shoulder. The weight of it startled me, but it was the most comforting thing I had felt in a long time from a woman. I was so tempted to kiss her forehead.

But that would breach her trust.

She snuggled further, getting comfortable on my shoulder as if it were a Savoir pillow. Instead of her forehead, my gaze shifted to her luscious lips, perfectly curved and inviting. They seemed to beckon me closer. Tempting me.

Thirteen

Aimee

I studied the two dresses on the bed. Which one would be more appropriate to meet Drago's in-laws? The soft blush or emerald green? Obviously, I don't want to send the message that we're in any kind of relationship except a professional one.

I held the two dresses up to me and tried to decide which one shouted conservative. Non-romantic. Colleague.

My cheeks burned, remembering waking up tucked into Drago's shoulder, thinking this plane provided some of the best firm but comfortable headrests. He did not even wake me. Furthermore, I went to sleep in his presence. The only time I sleep on a plane is when I travel with Topaz and her now extended family. Even when I fly private, I never *sleep*.

I apologized, wishing a hole would suck me out of the plane, but with a parachute stuck to my back. Not about to die from embarrassment, just escape. Drago didn't make it awkward, tilting the corner of his lips up and saying, "Now I can add a human pillow to my skill set."

After I woke, Drago ordered lunch. I sat straight in the chair, took out my tablet, and made notes on matters I wanted Leila to address. I kept myself busy for the remaining two hours of the flight, sitting fastened to my seat in the same spot, as if held in place by a large piece of Velcro.

I settled on the blush strapless dress with nude stilettos. Nude was my black; it goes with everything. I put my hair in a simple ponytail and kept my makeup light. Gathering my bag along with a gift for the bride-to-be, I took a deep breath, trying to calm my nerves.

Stepping out of my room, I looked down into the living area and my breath hitched in my throat. My eyes landed on Drago. He wore a natural-colored linen suit with a white shirt opened at the neck, and brown leather loafers. He glanced up at me and we stood there. Time stopped. My feet forgot how to work. The way the evening light framed him showing off the hint of auburn hues in his dark hair, his hazel eyes reflected specs that shined like gold nuggets...the more I studied him, the more my heart raced.

Trying to make light of the situation and break the tension—well, at least the tension from my end—I came down the stairs, walking toward him and tilting my head up to his six-foot-five frame. "If I ever launch a men's line, I have my first model."

"Ms. Patel, I'm certain you would not want me gracing your runway."

"Maybe you're right."

He guided me toward the front door, toward a waiting golf cart. The scent of the tropical flowers and the distant sound of waves crashing on the shore added to the surreal atmosphere.

He helped me into the cart, and after ensuring that I was safe, he got in and turned to me. "So, why wouldn't you have me on your runway?"

"That's for me to know and you to figure out."

Drago shook his head, a small smile playing on his lips. As we drove to the restaurant, the setting sun painted the sky with hues of orange and pink. I peeped at Drago from the corner of my eye. My clothing line was for everyday people. Drago looked Photoshop-ready without needing Photoshop.

Nothing about him said *everyday.*

Fourteen

Drago

Luna sat opposite us. Winter and her fiancé wore smiles that together would form a full circle, very much depicting the happy couple. The soft glow of the mini chandeliers above us cast a warm, intimate ambiance over the dinner table. The gentle murmur of conversations and occasional clinking of glasses added to the relaxed yet celebratory mood. Shifting her eyes toward mine, Winter said, "Do remember, the wedding rehearsal is tomorrow morning at 9:00 a.m. by the cabana on the beach."

Putting my fork down from the lobster crepe, which melted in my mouth, I savored the delicate flavors of the tender lobster mingling with the creamy richness of the sauce. The subtle hint of citrus and the fresh herbs added a burst of brightness, while the perfectly crisp edges of the crepe provided a satisfying contrast in texture.

My love for food meant I worked out six days a week to stay in shape. Even when I traveled, I stuck to my routine. Getting back on track demanded more discipline than staying on it—something I learned all too well after Minerva's death. In those early days, I barely had the will to do anything. It didn't seem real that she was gone. Her smile, her laugh, the warmth she brought into my life—how could all that just vanish? The only comfort I found was knowing she died doing what she loved. A massive heart attack took her while she was attending a conference, one where she was a featured speaker. A member of the hotel's housekeeping staff found her in her room, but by then, it was too late. She passed in her sleep.

Luna, placing her whiskey tumbler on the table, asked, "Aimee, what made you lug all this way? Because I know for sure you're not dating."

She waited longer than I expected before pouncing; we'd made it through introductions and the first course. A few more drinks and she would be slurring her words, revealing more than she intended.

Winter, trying to keep the peace, so like her aunt, said, "Aimee, thank you for the lovely gift. It's from your new line?"

Aimee nodded. "It's part of the Blue Orchid Intimates. I believe it is something both of you can enjoy."

Paul, Winter's fiancé, turned pink. From speaking with Winter, I gathered their wedding night would be the first time they would be intimate. Paul was a full-time youth pastor.

He came from a line of pastors, going all the way back to his great-great-grandfather.

Luna, of course, was not about to swayed off course. "Aimee, I hope you'll take no offense, because I like you—but you're not Drago's type. He likes older women. Minerva was eight years older. She was his professor. Like one of those romance novels, just in reverse."

Smiling, Aimee took a sip of her wine from the bottle that sat between us, which I opened after subtly showing her the still-sealed cork. "Drago is a colleague. We met a year ago when he stayed at one of our villas."

"Anyway, it's good to see that he has friends. He's probably celibate, knowing him. He's no fun. That body of his is wasted on him."

I held my breath as she took another sip of her drink, praying that Aimee's response would satisfy her and she would move on.

Resting her glass down, Luna continued. "He and Minerva were like Paul and Winter here, so in love. It was giddying watching them. There was no mistaking that he loved my sister." Raising her glass in the air, she declared, "To Minerva. I hope we meet again, but you're probably with angels. I'll more than likely join the devil and his imps in the afterlife."

Winter leaned over and removed her mother's glass, suggesting that she drink some water. Luna's date—who looked closer to seventy, speaking of age gaps—poured her a glass of water. I'm certain his bank account has at least one zero for every decade of life behind it. Luna somehow attracts rich older men. She and Minerva were so different. The same mother, but different fathers. Luna's father was an artist and Minerva's a scientist. That more than likely accounts for their differences. One thing, they loved each other.

Paul's parents, who observed the exchange with careful concern, seized this opportunity to officially welcome Winter to the family.

Dinner continued uneventfully, given Luna's presence and periodic drunken outbursts. The gentle flicker from the floating candles on the tables and the soft classical music playing in the background provided a counterpoint to the occasional tension.

After dinner, Aimee suggested walking back to the villa. The stars twinkled above us, and the breeze off the sea was cooling. The salty tang of the sea air mixed with the faint scent of tropical flowers, creating an intoxicating blend. Aimee hugged her arms against the cool breeze. Removing my jacket, I placed it over her shoulders. When my hand touched her skin, once again tiny shocks spiraled through my body, a reminder of the unexpected connection that seemed to build between us.

Pulling the jacket around herself, she said, "Thank you. Walking seemed like a good idea until we got outside, and that wind kicked up."

After that rich meal, I, too, welcomed the idea of the walk. We passed couples. Some held hands, others made out in the little cabanas on the beach, forgetting to close their privacy curtains, probably thinking no one could see them at this time of night. The sounds of the waves crashing gently against the shore and the occasional laughter of other guests created a serene and intimate atmosphere.

"Do you still miss her?" Aimee's voice was soft, almost hesitant.

Pushing my hands in my pockets, I replied, "Intelligent. Beautiful inside and out. The day I walked into my Personality Psychology lecture, my heart stopped. Her tanned skin glistened against the white dress she wore. Graduate classes are smaller, and because I was late, I had the seat closest to her desk. She had the loveliest brown eyes. The pull was almost instant. But nothing happened until I graduated. She was professional. The day after I graduated, I walked into her office and invited her to dinner."

Taking a deep breath and exhaling, I admitted, "I regret that my previous job involved so much traveling that I missed out on the time we had together. We got married when I was twenty-eight. She never nagged me about staying home or traveling too much. I bounced ideas off her to get a better understanding of people and their behaviors. Unknowingly or knowingly, she helped me solve some tough cases. I often wonder how different things would have been if I had spent more time with her."

Bumping me gently, Aimee said, "She sounds like an amazing woman."

"She was what I needed and more."

Fifteen

Aimee

Small, intimate wedding, my foot. Glancing around the wedding reception, there must have been close to two hundred people in attendance. For a destination wedding, getting here was not inexpensive, and furthermore, staying on this island—which was beyond five stars—added to the cost.

The speeches were over, kept short given that the after-ceremony photo shoot lasted over an hour. The guests did not complain as servers carried trays loaded with shrimp cocktail, bruschetta, cauliflower bites, and some local specialties I couldn't even name. From Dom Perignon to a plethora of non-alcoholic options, the bar was flowing. If I were eating and drinking, there was no way I would have room left to eat more.

This ballroom was impressive, with its high cathedral ceilings. I wondered if Topaz had seen pictures of this property. As I pondered this, Drago made his way through the crowd toward me. People parted, as if moved out of the way by some unseen force. Something about his swagger made me remember the first time I laid eyes on him. Topaz had been worried because, in nearly five years, he was the first man to elicit any reaction from me.

His complexion was a striking olive tone, a blend of his diverse heritage. He inherited his height from his Norwegian father, while his mother was African American. They met when his father moved to America. Interestingly, she was his boss. Well, his boss's boss, actually. She was the chief operations officer of the company that hired him to lead product design.

I only know all this because on the walk back to the villa the first night we arrived, he not only shared about his wife, but spoke lovingly about his family. He was an only child and close with his parents, who were retired and lived in Palm Beach, Florida.

Lifting my eyes to meet his, I said, "That was a moving speech. I like how you honored your wife and spoke from her perspective about what she would want for her niece."

"Ms. Patel, it seems I've finally done something you approve of. I could get used to this."

"Don't," I said, batting my lashes at him and smiling. "The happy mood of the wedding is obviously clouding my judgment."

He threw back his head and laughed. He looked so sexy... Some part of me wanted to give him more moments like that.

Continuing to keep my eyes on him, I said, "You should laugh more often."

He smiled and extended his hand, and said, "Let me guide you to our table. Dinner will be a four-course plated affair. I've asked for a bottle of wine to be stationed at our table unopened, along with a bottle of sealed sparkling water."

I squeezed the hand he held in appreciation. I wished he didn't have to go through all this because I couldn't get my head unstuck from the past. I so want to move on. I *need* to move on. This is an Anson property. I trust them, and I trust Drago.

As we were seated, I turned to him and said, "For tonight, I want to try. One glass of wine that is not opened in my presence. One glass of water that is not poured by me. Just tonight."

He nodded and called one of the servers. Dinner proceeded with fifteen-minute intervals between courses, filled with various musical pieces, including a rendition by a steel pan drummer that everyone loved. Leaning into Drago, I said, "I don't know how anyone is going to be able to dance after all this food. They might have to roll us all out of here."

"You know, they say children say the darndest things. I have a new take... Aimee says the darndest things."

After the dessert and the cake cutting, the couple had their first dance, followed by the father and daughter dance. There would be no lack of pictures; there were multiple photographers here and even some press photographers I recognized from previous shoots. Even so, I took a picture of Drago and Winter dancing. I had also taken one when he gave her hand in marriage and another when he made the speech that I'm sure did not leave a dry eye in the room, including his. I wasn't sure if he would ever get any of the photos being snapped by the professionals, and he deserved to have something to remember this special moment.

Drago appeared, extending his hand. "Just for tonight." My eyes remained fixed on his broad, strong hands, which carried scars and marks that reminded me he didn't always sit behind a desk and probably still doesn't all the time.

I hadn't danced in over five years. The thought of being held by a man again made my heart race. I'm certain sweat threatened to burst through my waterproof makeup, making a liar of the brand's claim.

Pushing back my chair, I took his hand. "Just for tonight."

Sixteen

Aimee

The room was the perfect temperature to get my final lazy moments before having to get dressed to leave. I snuggled further under the fluffy white duvet. The guests would typically give their checkout time when they book. But given the size of the group for the wedding and only the couple staying on for their honeymoon, we had until noon. Since I packed last night, that gave me a few more minutes, maybe another hour, to stay in bed. If Drago went for his morning run or workout, he would soon be back. The sun had already risen, peeking through the gap in the curtains. I never pull my curtains fully closed when I stay in a hotel. I love the sliver of light from outside filtering into the room.

Even though I was here through a barter arrangement of sorts, this was one of the best weekends I'd had in a long time. I didn't expect to enjoy it. Smiling, I recalled that I drank wine that wasn't opened in front of me, and water too. And I danced. Gosh, being pulled against Drago's body as we danced was far from awkward. Our bodies moved with ease as we found our rhythm, though I did accidentally step on his foot a few times. But with his arms around me, a sense of safety I hadn't experienced in years cocooned me. For those brief moments, how I ended up in this arrangement vanished from my mind. The only thing that remained was Drago, me, and the addictive feeling of peace.

The soft vibration of my cell phone pierced my thoughts. Tempted to ignore it, I remembered that Etim was five hours ahead. It could be an emergency, since it would be approaching noon there. My lips stretched into a smile as I grabbed the phone. "Tell me you did not get up to any trouble without me."

Topaz snorted. "I'm calling because you've been holding out on me."

Pulling the comforter more around me, I said, "You're right, I have been holding out. This place is gorgeous. You need to convince your mother-in-law to have the Christmas celebration here this year."

"Not that holding out."

"What are you talking about?" Still not ready to get out of bed, I thought about finding out everything about this bed, including the linen, and re-creating this experience at home. Although if I did, I might not get much work done. I guess that's why people come on vacation...- to experience something they don't in their everyday lives.

"You're plastered all over social media. Including the *Etim Chronicle*."

"What?"

"I love that off-the-shoulder silver mermaid dress you were wearing. And the shot where Drago's hand rested above the curve of your butt is so deliciously gossipy."

"Gossipy? Is that even a word? Are the baby hormones going to your brain?"

"Baby hormones, my foot. I can see that hand, and so do millions of other gossipy people. Listen to these few lines: 'Former Miss World and successful businesswoman Aimee Patel, who has never been photographed in public with a love interest, was captured dancing the night away with billionaire Drago Baas.' Want me to read more?"

"That social interest section of the paper is a total invasion of privacy."

"*Aimee.* You danced with Drago. Like, he *held* you."

"I know. It's crazy, right? In this weekend, I've made baby steps."

"Baby steps? That man's hand is resting above your butt! Giant leaps, it seems to me."

"Shut up." Heat flooded my cheeks; I didn't need a mirror to know my face turned a dusky rose against my golden-brown complexion. "Someone really needs to sue that newspaper."

Topaz laughed. "You looked happy, Aimee. Want me to send the picture?" I could hear the teasing in her voice.

"Absolutely not. It was an amazing weekend. Now, I need to get up and get ready. See you tomorrow."

The sun was up, and I heard movement downstairs; it was time to shower and grab a much-needed coffee. Standing and stretching, my phone vibrated again. That must be her sending me the picture. I would look at it after I showered and dressed.

Twenty minutes later, dressed in jeans and a blue button-down shirt, I grabbed my phone.

Coming down the stairs, Drago, dressed in khaki slacks and a white button-down, gazed up at me and said, "I was coming to knock to ensure that I did not dance you into unconsciousness."

Taking the orange juice he offered as I reached the last step, I replied, "Hard to say which of us is less used to dancing these days."

Wanting to give him a heads-up, I placed the glass on the table and said, "Topaz called. The *Etim Chronicle* has a picture from last night."

"I know. Luna had so many photographers around. Pictures were bound to be leaked."

Pulling out my phone to look at the picture from Topaz, I found it was not a picture but a message from an unknown number. As I read it, my stomach plummeted like someone bungee jumping without a rope.

"No! Nooo, nooooo!" I screamed.

The phone disappeared from my hands as Drago pulled me against him. The words on the screen ripped something loose inside me - I couldn't stop the sounds tearing from my throat, couldn't still my body.

Salt stung my lips as the first tear fell.

Then another.

And another.

Seventeen

Drago

Our departure was delayed by an hour. The resort island of ninety square miles had its own landing strip and tarmac that could accommodate a 747 or even an Airbus, along with a marina. Anson Island also had world-class medical facilities equipped with everything, even capable of performing emergency heart surgeries.

My eyes lingered on Aimee, her body still laid where I placed her after I lifted her onto the plane once the sedative took effect, stopping her body from shaking. Now, even in sleep, a frown occasionally creased her forehead, betraying the turmoil going on inside her mind. I couldn't help but guess the thoughts plaguing her subconscious, robbing her of a truly peaceful rest.

I sat on the bed, and, as if sensing my presence, her hand extended toward me. I held it to comfort her and maybe more to reassure myself that she was here, safe. Her soft grip was a small solace amid the chaos.

Before we boarded, I went through her phone and called Dr. Taitt, alerting her to make herself available to see Aimee. She replied, "If you believe it can't wait until tomorrow, I will come over."

"No, it can't. Thank you," I said, my tone leaving no room for disagreement.

Unlocking her phone, which only required her thumbprint, I scanned the messages which were sent earlier from an unknown number. My blood boiled with each line I read.

> How dare you let another man hold what is mine? You've always been mine. MINE.

> Sorry, you forgot. We've been apart too long. Know that I don't hold this against you. That was my doing.

> We'll pick up from where we left off all those years ago.

I've been watching. Your return to the runway was splendid. Sensational. I came all over myself. Look what you made me do. You should be punished for that.

No. That was me. You made me lose control. That is why I will punish you.

Seeing you reminded me of why I always wanted you. You owned the catwalk, and I owned you. I OWN YOU.

I was your first.

Your only.

Let's leave it like that.

You feel it too. That is why you never had another man.

Stop this foolishness. Don't start now. You would not like the consequences.

Sorry. Sorry.

It was hard seeing another man's hand on you like that. Only my hand should be on you.

Are you trying to embarrass me by having it all over the media? That's what you're doing? To get my attention? No, you're not like that?

Sorry.

But I was angry, seeing that man touching what's mine.

Still holding her hand, I studied the messages. The audacity of this man, the sheer delusion, made my hands tremble with rage. I wanted to find him, to make him pay for every threat, every word, for all the pain he caused Aimee.

When I get my hands on him, he will wish he was swimming with a hundred hungry sharks rather than facing me.

Eighteen

Aimee

The first sign of consciousness was the desperate need to empty my bladder. It willed me to open my eyes, but sleep and fogginess held onto me, unwilling to let me go, keeping me safe. The beds at this resort are amazing. There was something furry in the bed. At the bottom of the bed. Warm and furry. My eyes popped open. This was not the resort.

The messages. The memory rushed back to me, and I held my head, unable to process both the confirmation of what was done to me and the vile things he'd said.

"No. No. No," I whimpered.

Where am I? The last thing I remembered was Drago holding me. Comforting me. I remember speaking with a doctor. I wore the robe, which I took with me. Did Drago undress me?

Fear and confusion twisted inside me. Did something else happen? I struggled to remember more, but my mind was a blur.

Sitting up on the bed, the furry thing was a large black cat with gray eyes, the thick shaggy gray fur almost like a scarf around its neck. We stared at each other until it lost interest and began kneading the bed linens.

Where in heaven's name was I? Also, where was the bathroom?

As it turned out, finding the bathroom was not a challenge. My cosmetic bag rested on a glass countertop, which was a work of art with all its splashes of color. I studied my face after brushing my teeth; it was me, but half of my brain seemed to be replaced with cotton wool.

Lord. So tired.

The messages. Those messages. Drago saw the messages. Who else saw them?

Shame crawled into my brain, and dark thoughts replaced the cotton wool. How much had Drago seen? My private hell laid bare for him to judge. Now that I could at least function, I glanced around this room, seeing the small sitting area opposite the bed with two chairs and a small table overlooking what I knew to be Etim's city skyline. This had to be Drago's apartment or somehow connected to Drago.

When I walked out of the bathroom, the cat got up, stretched, and jumped off the bed, seemingly willing to be my guide, ensuring I did not get lost. Or maybe it was a nosy cat wanting to see what happened next. Stepping out of the bedroom, I heard voices. Familiar voices.

"Aimee is coming home with us. She got into this barter with you to help find out what happened, but she's my family. She's coming home with us," Topaz stated, her voice firm and unyielding.

"I can protect Aimee better here," Drago replied, his tone equally resolute.

Topaz was not backing down.

"Protect her from what? All you told us was she got messages, but you never said what they were about."

"Let Aimee decide," Shae interjected, trying to be the voice of reason.

The cat descended the stairs with its tail swishing from side to side; Drago's eyes followed his pet's movements.

Drago, Topaz, and Shae turned to look at me, as I perched hesitantly a few stairs from the bottom. Topaz rushed up to me. "Aimee!" She threw her arms around my neck, and we hugged.

"What time is it? Whatever time it is, I need something to eat. Maybe my brain will fully return so I can function."

Shae peeped at his watch. "It's going on 1:30 p.m. Let me take care of ordering food."

"While Shae does that, I'll have a fruit and vegetable platter set up and a selection of juices," Drago offered. "Coffee's already set up in the corner."

"That will work until the food arrives." I watched as Topaz went over and poured a cup of coffee for me. I wanted to ask Drago what happened after the messages, but I've never told my best friend—my sister—what happened, what caused me to return to Etim. She knew it was something, but not exactly what. It was all a poisonous substance bottled up inside of me that was slowly leaking out, destroying me from within. Those messages confirmed what I knew, but still didn't explain how. How did it all happen?

Shae. Topaz. Drago. Even the big, strange cat's eyes were on me. Their concern, so tangible I could retreat into it like a turtle in its shell and stay protected. Where do I start? Do I speak with Topaz first? But then I would have to repeat it all to Drago, because he's helping me. I don't have the energy to do that right now.

After I sat on the sofa, Topaz handed me a cup. Shae shook his head when she tipped her head in question toward the coffee pot. He said, "Instead of ordering, I will go and collect."

Topaz lifted her eyes to him. Those two were truly soul mates. They could communicate with a touch, unspoken words, or even a mere look. They could read each other and situations. Topaz nodded, and Shae left.

Nineteen

Aimee

After a slice of cantaloupe and two sips of coffee, my hunger subsided. I rested both items on the tray on the table in front of us. We've been through so much, but this one thing I've kept hidden. Topaz never pressed, and I never volunteered.

Not knowing what to do with my hands, I wrapped them around myself. Lord, where do I start? How do I even start?

Drago sat in a chair next to the sofa, and Topaz, placing her plate on the table, moved closer and hugged me. "You don't have to talk, Aimee. We are here for you. I'm here for you."

Drago got up. I sensed he was giving us space to talk, but I knew I could only do this once. I didn't have the mental strength to repeat myself and be questioned a second time.

This was it.

Holding Topaz's hand, I said, "Drago. Please stay."

"You're certain?"

Nodding, I replied, "I'm hoping to only share this once." Raising my eyes to meet his, I added, "If you have any questions, save them for later."

Sitting back down, he said, "Okay."

"Can you give Topaz the phone so she can read the messages?"

"Aimee, you don't have to," Topaz protested.

Squeezing her hand, I said, "It's easier if you read them. Then we can pick up from there."

Drago left the room and marched in the direction of what must be his home office. My eyes rested on the three large screens mounted on the wall. I assumed one of them must be a television. The house was void of any real character. Two abstract paintings hung on the walls. What he needed was a plant. Plants. Yes, I should give him a plant for all the trouble he went through. This was nothing he bargained for when he bartered with me to attend the wedding.

Drago returned. I reached out and placed my thumbprint on the phone to unlock it. He pulled up the messages and handed it to Topaz. She tried to control her expression, but I saw her eyes widen and the heave of her chest increase as she read the messages. Concern for her made me second-guess my plan; maybe letting her read the messages might not have been a good idea for the baby.

Touching her, I said, "Don't get worked up."

"How can I not get worked up? This person is sick."

As she wrapped her arms around me again, I closed my eyes, blocking out the hurt and pain I saw on Topaz's face. "Trust me. I know."

I pulled back to make eye contact with her, trying hard to block out Drago at this moment. A melancholic smile traced my lips. "You remember the pact we made before you went off to your internship in the Bahamas and me to the world of pageants to represent Etim?"

She nodded.

"I meant it, you know." A tear escaped and traveled down my cheek.

"Surely you know there is nothing that would impact how I see you?"

"That's the thing. In Paris, I dated no one. I wanted to wait for the 'one.' You wanted to wait until marriage. But given our different beliefs, I said in solidarity I would not sleep with anyone unless I knew he was the one—the one I would marry."

Topaz dropped our hands and kept her eyes trained on my face. "Some rich guy wanted a private showing for his wife and made a booking through the fashion house. I remember walking the show. I remember having a glass of champagne when we were done. But...but after that..."

Topaz hugged me once more; her warmth comforted me. "You don't have to continue."

"Yes, I need to get it out. It's killing me. Also, Drago needs to know everything if he is to help me." Turning to Drago, I said, "Can I have some water? Please."

I dreaded these next few minutes. *Lord, give me strength.* Drago returned with the glass of water and handed it to me. I took a sip. Taking the glass from him, I realized something astonishing: I *trusted* Drago. I was drinking something he gave me without seeing it come out from the tap or poured from a bottle.

Sipping the water and resting it on the coaster he'd placed on the table, I took another deep breath, trying to relax the tightness in my throat. I got one more sip of water and returned the glass to the table.

"One minute I was sipping champagne I grabbed off the tray. The next..." Swallowing and gripping Topaz's hand, I pressed on. "It was the next day, and I was back in my apartment. On my bed, in the same clothes I'd worn to the afterparty." Looking down at my feet, I forced out the next bit. "My panties were missing, though. And there were traces of blood between my legs."

Topaz's hands stilled. My words weighed down the atmosphere until it was too heavy to move. Drago clenched and unclenched his hands, almost like the calm before a storm.

"I called my fashion house. I did not tell them what happened, because I didn't *know* what happened. I suspected. But I told them I needed to go to a hospital. That was my first meeting with Dr. Dolos. You remember how I reacted when that trailer for the Chucky movie came on? Could not sleep for days. Her blue eyes reminded me of Chucky. She was so cold."

Glancing at both of them and dropping my eyes toward the water on the table, I said, "Dr. Dolos told me she could do a rape kit, but based on her years of experience, it looked consensual. She did blood work and had the gall to say I should be thankful that the person used a condom. She said I was *lucky*."

Drago snarled, "She's a piece of work. I hope she's not practicing anymore."

I gripped Topaz's hands. Tears pooled in my eyes. "My first time. My"—I took a deep breath and pushed the words out—"my *only* time, was not special. Not with that one. I can't even remember it."

Twenty

Drago

Sweat dripped off my body as I punched the bag. I couldn't get Aimee's story out of my head. No one deserved what happened to her. I wished this bag would fight back with me. At first, I thought she was young, stupid, drank too much until she blacked out. The more I looked, though, the more I suspected something. But not this. Whatever this was, it was well orchestrated. This person had connections and power to cover their tracks.

"Listen, if you split that bag, I will have nothing to train with," Jaden said, his tone reprimanding.

I converted the underground floor into both parking and a state-of-the-art gym, along with a vault that carried special supplies we needed for our work. I ensured that our homes had safe rooms and weapons.

Turning my head to him, I smiled. He was already putting on a pair of gloves. "I see you want to go a round with me."

"I'm going to teach you a lesson for abusing the bag. Man, the thing can't defend itself."

"You sure you want to go a round with me? I'm not in the best frame of mind."

Shaking his head, he replied, "You have the best control, no matter what. Remember the last mission? We were surrounded. Ten men to us in the hut. I wanted to go out guns blazing because I thought we were going to die. But you came up with a plan. Unfortunately, it involved pushing ourselves into a hole we dug to keep our weapons and supplies hidden. You blew up most of the house, killing half the men. They didn't think we were still alive, so when we emerged, we were able to take out the remaining."

Shifting on his feet, Jaden asked, "Ready?"

He didn't wait for me to answer. Sneaky Jaden threw the first punch. We made a promise when sparring, no headshots. We went at it for another forty minutes before we called it quits.

Sitting on the floor, I asked between heaving breaths, "The job. Completed?"

Glancing up at the clock on the wall, he nodded. "Within another six hours. "What's up? I haven't seen you so tightly wound up in a long time," Jaden added, flashing his perfect white teeth. "A *woman*?"

"Shut up before I knock out your teeth and Tanisha comes to hunt me down." Jaden's wife, Tanisha, with her soft-spoken voice, was lethal with her words—and dangerous in her own right. She was a botanist, and Jaden's go-to when we needed a little something for a job. I keep on her best side at all times.

"Scared of her, too?" Jaden smirked. We laughed.

"You would never think someone so small could be so terrifying," I said, raising my water bottle to my mouth.

Jaden reached for his. "So, it's a woman?"

Closing my eyes, I sighed. "Aimee Patel."

Twenty-One

Aimee

Topaz insisted I stay with them, but I convinced her that remaining at Drago was best for me.

As I sipped my coffee, I scanned the books in Drago's library. *The Gift of Fear* caught my eye with its interesting title. The entire section on criminal profiling intrigued me. My gaze landed on a book I recognized. I had watched the movie, but never read the book. Tracing my fingers over *The Bourne Identity*, I decided I might borrow it and read it for the few days I was here. It was good to have choices when it came to distractions—Not that I didn't have enough work to do. In ten minutes, I had a call with Leila and then an appointment with Dr. Taitt; she agreed to another house visit, which I was anxious about.

I set up my tablet for the conference call. While I wanted to go with Topaz, I could not be selfish. Besides actively involved in the completion of the Anson Resort, she continued to serve as the representative for Needhams, focusing on attracting investment to the area. She also needed to take care of herself and the baby and not add to her stress by worrying about me. Not knowing fully what we were truly facing, I wanted to keep any danger away from her.

Drago's desk was a clash of old-world charm and contemporary design, with legs made of intricate wood carvings and the top made of glass. The combination worked beautifully. I slid into the large black chair, which complemented the furnishings in the room. I was like Goldilocks in Papa Bear's chair; it must have been custom made for his long frame.

When I joined the conference call link, Leila was already waiting. "Morning, Leila."

"Morning," she replied, still fiddling with something on her end. "Give me a minute; trying to share the report."

"My bad, I forgot to give you permission to share."

"Ohhh."

For the next twenty minutes, I received updates on the status of our orders. Leila was also in contact with our manufacturer in Portugal.

"Leila, organize a visit for us."

"You want me to come?" Her eyes were wider than the large button securing my wrap dress at the waist.

"Yes, I'll send you the details to arrange the plane. Let them know it will be a same day return trip. I prefer the same crew I normally use, if they are available."

"How soon?" Her brows now squished together.

"Friday. Problem?"

"No, not really." Holding her phone in her hand, she said, "I did not mention in the interview, but I'm a reserve in the military. Once a month, we have drill training. Because I also train on surveillance equipment, that's twice a month for me." She rushed on. "I didn't mention it as I was excited about getting the job. Also, you indicated that weekend work would seldom be required. Sorry. The next two Fridays I must report at 1600 hours."

Leila, in the military? She loves pink. *Really* into pink. Pink Michael Kors bag with matching pink MK umbrella. Even on her right ring finger sat a chunky rose quartz ring, which she made. I remembered to shut my mouth, so I wouldn't resemble a fish.

"The training this weekend was only arranged last week. But I'd love to accompany you to see the clothing production first-hand," she said, her eyes sparkling with excitement.

"I will ensure that you're back in time." Shaking my head in wonder, I asked, "How long were you in the military?"

"Served straight from eighteen. Did the first term full time. The military paid for my degree, hence business with a minor in fashion. My parents could not afford to send me to university, and being the first person in my family to have a degree was a dream of mine. But I continue to serve because they have been good to me." There was a catch in her voice. "Plus, I love working with the surveillance equipment. And the drills keep me fit. Once a year, I have annual training for two weeks, but I will take that as vacation."

"No such thing. You will have that as paid leave."

Her eyes grew wide. "Really? You're racking up boss of the year points. Let me go and arrange the visit."

"Don't alert them we're coming. I want to see their standard practices. They assured me they treat their staff ethically. The previous times I visited were all arranged by them."

"Gotcha."

Drago

Being pummeled by Jaden this morning helped clear my head. Pulling Aimee's file, my hand quivered over the keys. *Get out of your head, Drago.* If I want to help Aimee, I have to pull my act together. Her words, her voice, her tears as she spoke rolled around in my head all night. She tried to be brave when Shae returned with the food, but after listening to Aimee, the rage building in me swallowed up any appetite for food and created a need for vengeance. I couldn't shake the image of her tear-streaked face, the way her voice trembled yet held a determined edge.

Focusing on the small, round conference room table in front of me, I gave myself one final shake, exhaled, and updated the file. *Don't think. Enter the information so you can process it later.*

I'm going to speak to Bishop. We're going to take this case. Aimee deserves justice, and I won't let my emotions get in the way.

I could try to fool myself and say she's a client, but I'm too old for that. Last year, when I first saw her with Topaz—and the ridiculously large gift basket—a faint jolt flickered through me. But I shut it down so quickly, turning it off like I would a tap. Unfortunately, I did not tighten it sufficiently, because Aimee Patel has leaked into the fabric of my life in the short time we'd been together. Knowing she was working from my home office gave me peace of mind. But the truth hit me like one of Jaden's punches. Resting my head back on the chair and pinching the bridge of my nose, I realized I liked knowing she was in my home. There was a comfort in knowing she was minutes away.

Man, I have it bad.

Taking a deep breath, I tried to focus on the tasks ahead. As I organized my thoughts for the day, the door pushed open and Jaden entered, disrupting my concentration. He turned on the TV located near the entrance of the door and which faced my desk.

"Breaking news story!" the reporter's voice announced with urgency. "The Global Finance Consortium member for developing countries, Edwin Campbell, collapsed and died on his first day reporting to work after a holiday in Greece. He was entering the elevator to take him to his office when he collapsed."

Jaden turned off the television and left.

Twenty-Two

Drago

The elevator slid open, and I pressed my thumb on another door, reinforced to withstand a bomb blast. The second door, resembling the elevator, slid open. In our line of work, precaution was as necessary as sunshine. Sebastian's bed was empty. My aloof cat was not here to give me the onceover and find me lacking.

It was 6:00 p.m., and I needed to find out what Aimee wanted to eat. There were meals Stacey prepared that we could reheat, or we could order takeout. Aimee messaged, asking what time I would be home. For a moment, it was as if I was in a choke hold. Whether I came or went in the last five years made no difference to anyone. Not since Minerva. Bishop and Jaden cared, but no one *checked* on me. Sebastian wouldn't even if he could.

As I passed the floor-to-ceiling windows with the sun still high in the sky due to the season, the rich aromas of garlic, curry and other herbs floated toward me. Stacey could cook, but this was not one of her standard meals. Following the mouthwatering trail, I entered the kitchen. On one of the stools surrounding the large island sat Sebastian. Traitor.

Aimee wore a yellow cotton dress. I recalled seeing her lounging in it while we were at the villa on Anson Island. Lifting her eyes toward mine as she replaced a cover on the pot, she said, "I wanted to do something to say thank you." I raised a brow at her as she continued. "For everything. After the messages. Even yesterday, I could barely function."

Taking off my jacket, I thought better of draping it on the back of the stool Sebastian occupied. I would not put it past him to stick his claws in it for disturbing his rest and time with his new favorite person.

Traitor.

Unbuttoning and rolling up my shirt sleeves, I said, "I need no thanks."

"Well, we need food," Aimee replied.

"No argument there. Let's eat on the patio outside." Reaching above her, I took down the cast iron plates and slid them in the oven to heat. "Give me ten minutes to shower and change."

Turning, we collided. I grabbed her upper arms to keep her from falling, and she mumbled, "Sorry. I wanted to see the temperature you set on the oven."

My hands remained on her arms. Her skin reminded me of the silk dress that she wore to the wedding.

I looked into her silver-gray eyes. "175 degrees Fahrenheit."

"What?"

"The temperature for the cast iron plates."

A deep flush colored her cheeks. "Yes. Thanks."

Removing my hands, I said as calmly as I could, "Give me a few minutes. The oven will beep, but leave them in. The longer they are in there, the more heat they will retain when we dine outside."

Leaving the kitchen, I reflected on the message and now a home-cooked meal. Don't forget her skin. Those eyes. How she smells. How am I going to get through this evening? A quick shower will settle everything. Especially the pressure against my zipper.

Minerva was the one who was the Christian in our relationship. I attended church with her, the sinner the pastor was set on saving. Even after all these years, the pastor still sent me a card at Christmas, and every year I send a monetary donation to the church.

So, Minerva's God, don't let me do anything stupid. Please. The pressure against the zip did not ease.

After showering and dressing in jeans and a white T-shirt, I gave myself a good pep talk and steeled my nerves, ready to face Aimee Patel in all her glory.

After entering the kitchen, I removed the plates from the oven. Aimee opened the pots. She served a creamy mash with curried chicken, mushrooms, and steamed vegetables. Returning the pot to the stove, she said, "I wasn't sure if you were allergic to shellfish, so I went with chicken. It seemed safer. Plus,

I've not had this in a while. It brings back memories of Maa. It was my favorite meal growing up. The only thing missing is naan bread."

I'm such a goner for this woman. If she had cooked shellfish and I was allergic, I would have eaten it with a side of antihistamines and prayed I did not die.

Resting the plates on a tray, I said, "Grab a bottle of wine. Your choice."

Watching her furrow her brows as she scanned the large selection, I glanced at Sebastian, who was giving me what can only be described as the evil eye. I stuck my tongue out at him. *Drago, are you seriously competing with the cat for Aimee's attention?*

Knowing Aimee, the odds were probably in Sebastian's favor.

She selected a bottle and grabbed the wine glasses. I escorted her to the patio. I shot Sebastian a smirk as we went outside. "Oh, it's beautiful," she said.

Uncorking the wine, I nodded. "It is." The lights twinkled from a few buildings that were taller than this one. Etim doesn't allow skyscrapers. "The last time I was out here was when this furniture was delivered."

Taking a bite of the food, I said, "This is delicious. Am I getting a hint of coconut? You don't strike me as the cooking type."

"Wrong. I don't love cooking, but I can cook. Yes, there is some coconut milk in the curry sauce. Topaz and I often rotated preparing meals, especially breakfast."

As Aimee gazed out at the sky, the wind played with the strands of her hair. I wanted to broach something with her but was concerned it might not go over well. I didn't know how long she planned on staying, but I would feel better if she went along with what I was about to propose.

"Given all the medals Topaz won representing Etim, I bet she's a better shot than most snipers. What about you?"

"Not in Topaz's range, but I do own a gun."

My brows rose at that little fact. "Do you go to the range?"

"I haven't practiced in a while."

Resting my hand on the table, I continued. "I don't know what we're dealing with." Pausing and resting my hand on hers, I said, "Before you think of returning home, I want you to undergo defensive training. Including firearms."

"How long? I'm traveling to Portugal on Friday but returning the same day."

My heart sped up at this news, although she mentioned she would return the same day.

"Leila is arranging the trip."

"Take my plane. I would feel safer."

"Okay. I will get her to organize payment."

I'm not taking her money. Now I have to find a reason to return the first payment. I don't think we're ready for that discussion.

"Defensive training. How long?"

"Can't wait to be rid of me?" I asked, draining the last few drops of wine that remained in the glass.

"I have my greenhouse. Although everything is automated, I still need to periodically check on my plants. The good thing is we have long-term rentals at the villas. But all the samples for my line are in my office. Leila works remotely, but the plan is for us to work together in person two days per month."

"We will figure it out. But until we know more, I would rather you don't return home."

"Two weeks," Aimee said. "At home, I have an excellent security system. My home is my sanctuary. There are renters around. Not exactly isolated. Plus, all these years, this person never contacted me. Maybe they wanted to scare me."

That was the worrying part. Why now, after all these years? No, this person wanted more than to scare her. But I wasn't going to bring that up yet.

We talked and laughed. We drank the entire bottle of wine. Honestly, I couldn't recall the last time I relaxed and enjoyed a good meal.

Years.

The sun had long set, and the temperature dropped. We stood to go inside. Biting back a yawn, Aimee said, "My bed is calling me."

"Go on up. I will take everything in."

We stood. She paused, lifting her eyes to meet mine, rose on her toes and grazed a kiss to my cheek. I watched her walk up the steps, followed by the bloody cat. I swore he winked at me.

Twenty-Three

Aimee

While I wanted to surprise the company, turning up totally unannounced was still not my style. Leila called when we landed and informed them about our visit. The production area was cool. Ladies of all ages, the youngest appearing to be in their mid-twenties, to the supervisor, who could be in her sixties, were working diligently. There were a few gentlemen who appeared to be more focused on the production of men's garments.

"Mariana?" She tilted her head up toward me. "We would also like to do a quick inventory check while we're here."

"Of course, Ms. Patel."

"Aimee."

"Ms. Costa, this is the full list of items we wish to check," Leila said, papers in outstretched hand.

Today, Leila was dressed fully in black, her telltale pink added by the ballerina flats she wore. The inventory check took us over an hour. Mariana was accommodating, despite our short notice. Blue Orchid brand was not only for the everyday woman, but being produced by women for women in an ethical manner was important for the brand. I would never want to exploit anyone to make a dime.

As we were leaving, I said, "Mariana, thank you again. I wanted to do a spot check. Can't promise it will be the last time."

"Aimee, until you are comfortable with our partnership, you're always welcome." She clasped my hands in hers, her smile reaching her eyes.

When I met with her and her father a year ago, it was clear this was both a business and family affair. The conference room displayed mementos of the company's history— awards, old photographs, and handwritten notes of appreciation from long-time clients. Again, that was projected in the atmosphere as we walked the production floor. Employees worked diligently, but there was easy chatter and laughter among them.

The visit to Costa's Apparel confirmed I made the right choice. I knew I would make mistakes along the way, but I wanted to minimize them as much as possible.

"Leila, seeing you've never been here, I would be a mean boss if we didn't at least stroll the Ribeira and have lunch at one of the cafés."

After thirty minutes of walking along the riverside and observing the bustle of tourists, we settled on a café. The sun was warm on our backs, and the sound of the Douro River flowing nearby added a peaceful ambiance to our stroll.

Opening her menu, Leila said, "This reminds me so much of Etim, yet different."

"How?"

"More hints of old European charm. Etim is modern and cosmopolitan."

After we ordered, she glanced at her watch and I said, "Trust me, you will be back in time for your training. I would never have pegged you as someone in the military."

The server placed two glasses of water on the table. I said, "Sorry, can we have a bottle of water for the table, unopened?" The server nodded amicably and removed the glasses to return with empty ones and the requested bottle of water.

"I normally enjoy it," Leila said.

"Not anymore?"

Shrugging, she replied, "My regular commanding officer was reassigned last month. We were introduced to his replacement. He doesn't seem as approachable. The military...it's a team. Maybe I don't like change." Sipping her water, she seemed to shake off the reservations. "I'm rambling. Anyway, he's not really our officer; he's here mainly on special assignment and overseeing our surveillance training." Taking another sip of the water, she mumbled, "I can't wait for him to go."

"I see. Do you have other part-time work?" I asked.

"No. I do some virtual assistance contracts. And my jewelry."

The server returned with our orders. We had both ordered soup, and I recommended a *bifana* for us to share, so Leila could sample this popular Portuguese sandwich, which I absolutely loved. It's thinly sliced, marinated pork served in a crusty roll. The rich aroma of the soup and the savory scent of the bifana filled the air, making my mouth water.

While I waited for the bill, Leila called our driver. Walking to our pickup point, my phone buzzed. Topaz and Drago knew I was in Portugal. There were orders that were set to ship today. We checked, double- and triple-checked yesterday. Lord, please don't let there be a problem. Pulling out the phone, I saw a message from an unknown number. A shiver ran down my spine. My hand trembled.

"Aimee. Are you okay?"

I clicked on the message.

Hope you're enjoying Portugal.

Blue suits you.

It reminds me of your launch. Oh yes, I was there.

You forgot to invite me. How naughty of you!

Twenty-Four

Drago

We'd been training for at least thirty-five minutes. I watched her as she drank water. Sweat dripped down her face, and her chest rose and fell. The combination of the air conditioning and her perspiration made the peaks that pressed against the fabric of her workout top obvious.

Shaking my head, I chastised myself.

Focus.

When I woke this morning, Aimee was already dressed in gym clothes. Yesterday, when she returned, she said, "We're starting training tomorrow." She had two bags, which I guessed were from shopping. She said nothing about the message she forwarded to me.

When I read the message, a sense of helplessness settled around me. It brought me back to when I first heard about Minerva's death. I never expected to feel such hopelessness again. A roar came out of me that sent Jaden barreling into my office.

Aimee had crept under my fence and set up camp. The thing is, I didn't want to kick her out.

She was miles away. I could have done nothing. The app I installed on her phone, designed for use only by government-authorized agencies, pinged the number that had sent her the message as being in Colombia, Alaska, New Zealand, and São Tomé and Príncipe, a small island on the equator. But none of them placed her predator anywhere near Portugal. He had access to serious resources. But we were better.

"Ready?" I asked.

She nodded.

"One more thing we're going to work on today is escaping a chokehold. Tomorrow, we'll review everything we did today. Next week, we'll start on your target practice."

Aimee stepped onto the mat.

I positioned myself behind her. "I'll apply a light chokehold. Stay calm and follow my instructions."

Gently, I wrapped my arm around her neck. Aimee tensed briefly, then relaxed.

"Tuck your chin down to protect your throat." Once she had done that, I said, "Grab my arm with both hands to create space."

She gripped my arm firmly. "Next, turn your body slightly and step behind my leg for leverage."

Aimee twisted her body and positioned her foot as directed. "Perfect. Now, use your elbow to strike my ribs and push down on my arm."

With a swift motion, Aimee jabbed her elbow into my side and pushed down. I released my hold, stepping back with a smile. She learned quickly. What I admired most was that no matter how difficult it was, she never complained.

"Let's do that again," I said.

Twenty minutes later, we were both sitting on the floor, Aimee's breathing labored.

"You barely broke a sweat. I feel like every muscle in my body is screaming at me, wanting to know what they've done to deserve this."

"You, Ms. Aimee Patel, are what we call out of shape."

Bouncing me with her shoulder, she said, "Thank you for informing me. Guess I wouldn't have figured that out, given that I don't think I can move."

Pointing toward the treadmill, I said, "Tomorrow, we're going to start with cardio. Thirty minutes."

She sipped her water, her breathing slowing.

Aimee rested her hand on my thigh. "Yesterday," she said, turning to face me, "the first thing that surged through me was fear. But then I balled my fists, wishing I could get my hands on this person."

I did not want to bring up the message until she was ready to talk about it. Now that she did, there was something in the message that bothered me. Well, the entire message bothered me, but something specific stood out.

"I need to ask you a few questions."

Aimee focused on me as she continued to sip her water.

"He mentioned seeing you. Who handled security at your launch?"

"Holly. She works for Shae's sister, Sapphire."

Standing in one motion and extending my hand to pull up Aimee, I said, "We need to call her."

"You must show me how to get up like that."

"That requires core muscles."

She rolled her eyes at me.

Laughing, I said, "Come on, let's go upstairs and make that call."

Holly confirmed that only attendees on the list were allowed in. As Holly remained on the video call, I said, "What if he was able to see but wasn't there?"

Holly raised a brow. "Not possible. That was an interior room with no windows. Doors opened to a corridor."

Leaning forward, something from the night of the launch rushed to my memory. "How did Topaz view the launch?"

"I set up a camera for her."

"So, she didn't need to hack into the resort's surveillance system?"

Her brow furrowed and she shook her head. So, it wasn't Topaz. It was him.

Twenty-Five

Aimee

The marina, with its super yachts docked, was a sight to behold. Topaz and I stopped to purchase ice cream and sat on one of the benches. Her security detail had been instructed not to let us out of their sight. Shae increased her security since the messages. Maybe until everything was resolved, we should keep our contact to phone and video calls.

"Knock, knock. Aimee, you there?"

I glanced toward Mark and the other member of her security detail. "It's obvious Shae believes that whatever is unfolding around me poses an increased risk."

"Shae is just being Shae—over-the-top protective."

"But he's right." I continued to lick my double chocolate-chip ice cream. "This person is obviously well connected, and it's scary. We don't know what they're capable of."

"Don't forget—psychopath," Topaz added, her tone more serious now.

"Psychopath. A billion percent certifiable psychopath." Finishing my cone, I added, "With the baby and all, I don't want anything to happen to you. Maybe we should limit our public outings and contact. If he came after you..."

"I would shoot him. I wouldn't even apologize. I'm certain I wouldn't ask God to forgive me. I believe God would consider it a public service for taking this psycho off the streets."

I chuckled, appreciating her fierce loyalty. "Yes, vigilante. Please stop watching Batman reruns."

"If you're worried, we'll be extra careful. Plus, the doctor has cleared me to travel. We'll be spending a month in Miami to begin planning for the opening; also, Shae needs to attend board meetings."

The evening sun reflected off the water, casting a golden glow. People jogged on the boardwalk, oblivious to the turmoil in my life. This unknown entity could be out here, and we wouldn't even know. The thought sent a shiver through my body. "It's been over two weeks since the first message, and we're no closer to figuring out who this person is. I can't continue to stay with Drago."

"You certainly can't go home. Especially with us traveling at the end of the week. Unless Drago is complaining, that's the safest place for you."

"I kissed him."

Her mouth formed the perfect O. "What?"

"Nothing like that. On his jaw last week. To say thanks."

"Aimee, that's...good?"

I shrugged, feeling a mix of confusion and longing. "I'm attracted to him. But I don't—" My voice trailed off, unsure of how to articulate my muddled feelings.

"What's going through that mind of yours?"

In the last five years, I have never experienced desire. The attraction, or pull to the opposite sex, was not there. I was around some men that persons might pinch to see if they were real because they were so gorgeous, but they did nothing to me or for me. A nervous laugh escaped my lips. "I'm an excellent actress. I can act sexual, but no one made my skin tingle. Until now."

Turning my head toward Topaz, I asked, "How do I even know if I'd really allow him to touch me like a man would touch a woman?"

"Well, his hands were all over you in that picture from the wedding," she pointed out, raising a brow.

On one of the yachts, a crew was cleaning. I watched as they moved the furniture around. On another there was a party of some sort, with servers moving around offering food and drinks.

"Aimee," Topaz called, breaking my reverie.

Shaking my head, I said, "The wedding was public. People were around. It was safe. But can I be normal? Would I be able to, you know..."

"Have sex? Make love?" she finished for me, her voice gentle.

I nodded. A lump formed in my throat.

"Do you want to?"

"Not now. But I believe normal people do that. I want normal. I'm tired of this life," I confessed, the words coming out more urgently than I intended.

"You want normal with Drago?" She leaned in, her eyes searching mine.

Sitting up, I said, "I want normal for Aimee. I want my life back. Every aspect."

Biting my lip, I thought about what Dr. Taitt had suggested earlier in the week. It was a lot to consider, and I wasn't sure I was ready.

"I spoke to Dr. Taitt about this."

Topaz narrowed her eyes, concern evident on her face. "And?"

Letting out a breath, "It's not her area of expertise. She gave me a referral." Taking another deep breath, I pushed the words out. "For a sex therapist."

Topaz's mouth fell open once more.

Twenty-Six

Drago

Aimee adjusted her stance. Over the last three weeks, her endurance had improved, and her breathing was steady. She was becoming more confident, and I could see the determination in her eyes.

Holding up padded mitts, I said, "One last time, and we call it quits. Remember, exhale as you strike and use your whole body."

Aimee nodded, her focus sharp. She took a deep breath, then stepped forward, driving her palm into the mitt with a sharp exhale. The impact was solid, a satisfying thud that sent a jolt through my arm.

"Great job," I said, lowering the mitt. "That was perfect."

Aimee smiled, a mix of pride and relief on her face. "Between Topaz and you, I could be a killing machine."

I grinned, touching her nose with the mitt. "You mean you and Topaz are double trouble?"

"Take that back!"

I chuckled and turned my back to move away. Suddenly, Aimee executed a foot swipe, catching me off guard and sending me tumbling to the ground. Unfortunately for her, she lost her balance as well and fell with me. I quickly rolled over, pinning her beneath me, still smiling. The thrill of her progress, combined with the heat of her body against mine, sparked a protective instinct. But there was also something deeper.

"I did it! I got you down. Wait till I tell Jaden," she gloated, her voice full of excitement.

"You're going to tell Jaden?" I repeated, my eyes dropping to her lips. The temptation to kiss her was overwhelming, but I fought it. Her silver eyes searched my face, her pupils dilated with either excitement or fear. The thought of scaring her made me pull back slightly. "You get bragging rights. If you ever get in this position, play dirty. Your aim is to escape. Hit them in the eyes, throat, groin. You might only get one chance. Make it count."

She blinked, then nodded, her expression serious.

Getting up, I pulled her to her feet. "Time to feed the trainer," I said, trying to shake off the moment. I was certainly hungry, though what I wanted wasn't on the menu.

After she grabbed her towel and water bottle, we moved toward the elevator. "You know, Sir Trainer, there won't be anything special for dinner tonight. Just warmed-up leftovers from last night and a Greek salad."

She was so wrong. Once she was here, it was special. Sometimes, instead of eating at my desk, I came home for lunch. Before having her here, I didn't realize how empty my place was—how empty my life was without her in it.

The doors slid open, revealing Sebastian sitting right in front of the entrance, ready to guard Aimee as if he was a Rottweiler. Aimee bent down to tickle him, and he immediately rolled over, baring his belly.

"Hey, big boy. We're going to grab a shower, then we'll all eat."

Yup, even the cat eats when we're eating. Stacey can put out food, but the cat ignores it unless Aimee gives him his special treat. Breakfast is dry food; dinner is the salmon dish. The funny thing is, Aimee doesn't eat salmon, but she read that cats love it. Hence, the inseparable bond between the two.

Aimee went upstairs and left her door ajar, knowing the cat would follow.

She's cast a spell on both of us. Shaking my head, I sauntered to my room. When I returned, Aimee said she wanted to dine outside. The plates were already in the oven. Sebastian licked the contents of his container, purring in appreciation. Whenever we ate outside, she fed Sebastian first.

I grabbed a bottle of Santa Margherita Pinot.

The oven beeped, and Aimee plated the food. I took the salad from the fridge. Once she set up outside, I returned for the wine and glasses.

Tonight, before we ate, she blessed the meal. We're not consistent. Minerva always prayed before meals. Aimee said her spiritual influence came from Topaz and Topaz's parents. She hasn't mentioned much about her own family. Both her parents were dead; maybe it was a sore point.

"You're quiet," she said.

Sipping my wine, I replied, "Thinking."

"About?"

"You don't talk much about your parents."

She studied her wine and finished a bite. "I loved my parents. Thinking about them creates mixed feelings." She glanced out at the skyline, then got up and went and stood by the railing.

Leaving the table, I stood beside her. The wind carried her sweet, powdery scent, stirring a pang of something long buried within me. She shivered, despite wearing a sweater. I moved behind her and caged her in with my arms to give her warmth while resting my chin on her head. The closeness was intoxicating, yet it was natural, like she belonged there.

"Show-off. You're reminding me you're a giant."

Laughing, I closed the space a little between us as we continued to stare at the skyline.

"I never understood the fascination of living in the city. I love looking out at the skyline—it's beautiful. But I still prefer Needhams. Thinking of my parents reminds me of how alone

I am in this world. But I'm grateful for another family God blessed me with—Topaz, and all that comes with her. I love her parents and her in-laws." Leaning into me, she added, "They treat me like one of them."

We stood there, listening to the distant hum of traffic and the night noises. The day's stress dropped off me, and for a moment, everything in my orbit was right.

"Drago," Aimee whispered, as if not wanting to disturb the moment. "You reluctantly took on my case. Now I'm here at your home for three weeks. I want you to be upfront with me. Anytime you need your space or need me to leave, please tell me. The last thing I want is to be a burden to anyone, especially you."

She turned and tilted her head toward me. I said, "I might not have wanted to take this case, because, honestly, I thought there was no case. But I'm glad I did. If you weren't here, I'd be worried, getting more gray hair by the second."

"You have gray hair?"

"At thirty-nine, with the work I do? Yup."

My eyes rested on her lips again, the urge to kiss her growing stronger. But something caught my attention. Pulling my gaze away from Aimee and staring into the night sky, I muttered, "What the hell?"

Twenty-Seven

Drago

"Go inside. Don't run. Walk with purpose." Tapping my watch, I barked, "Call Jaden."

"What's up, old—"

"Get your Remington and high-magnification scope. We have a drone. When you step out on the patio, you'll see it. Shoot it down. Now."

"On it."

If not for the light from another building reflecting off it, I would have missed it. The drone hovered there in the darkness, its black silhouette almost invisible against the night sky. A chill ran down my spine; whoever was operating it knew exactly what they were doing. It was unsettling to think about how close they could be, watching us without our knowledge.

"Boss. Ready."

"Check to ensure there are no explosives. Then shoot it down."

"No explosives."

Was this connected to us? Or was this about Aimee? My gut twisted, leaning toward the latter. This person had upped their game, and the fact they knew where I lived was unsettling. I had a penthouse registered under my name nearby, but they were targeting this place.

Two shots rang out, echoing in the still night air.

"Boss, I'm going down to collect what evidence I can."

"I'm coming."

I closed the door and pressed the button to shut the drapes, trying to keep my composure. Inside, my thoughts raced. Whoever was after Aimee wasn't playing games; they were serious, and that scared me more than I cared to admit. The responsibility of keeping her safe weighed heavily on me.

Aimee's voice trembled as she asked, "What's going on?"

I turned to her. Her hands clutched the fabric of her sweater, tendons stark across her knuckles. Her eyes were wide, reflecting a mixture of fear and resolve. The usual calm in her demeanor was replaced by a subtle tremor in her voice, betraying her anxiety.

"I spotted a drone outside. Jaden brought it down. I'll be back in a few."

Aimee nodded, her lips pressed into a thin line. She took a deep breath, trying to steady herself, but I could see the flicker of unease in her gaze. Her body language was tense, her shoulders hunched slightly as if bracing for bad news. Despite her efforts to appear composed, the slight quiver in her hands gave her away.

It took Jaden and me at least an hour to check everything. When I returned, Aimee sat on the stairs, stroking Sebastian. The cat looked as concerned as she did, his tail twitching nervously and ears perked, sensing the tension in the air. She looked up as I approached, her face a mask of determination, but the worry lines around her eyes were unmistakable.

Sitting next to her, I pinched the bridge of my nose, trying to think clearly. Lord, we're running around in circles and getting no closer to whoever is after Aimee. "We're missing something. But trust me, we'll figure it out. I want you to minimize the time you spend outside. These windows are bulletproof. Bishop and I designed the remodel of this building to withstand most attacks."

Blinking at me, she asked, "What about my meeting with Leila next week? I keep rescheduling." Her voice was steadier now, but there was a trace of frustration. Aimee hated feeling powerless, and the constant rescheduling was clearly wearing on her.

I wished this would all be resolved by next week, but each day, another layer was revealed. It was like trying to solve a puzzle with half the pieces missing. That drone wasn't amateur equipment. Despite the two shots Jaden fired, when we reached the back of our building, most of the drone was still intact. Very few people have drones built from that kind of material.

No, we're missing something. Something that ties all this together. The precision, the resources—it all pointed to someone who was serious and capable.

"When you go to meet Leila next week, Jaden or I will be going with you." Pushing to my feet, I added, "None of this makes sense."

Aimee looked up at me, her expression a mixture of gratitude and unease. She nodded then averted her gaze, biting her lower lip. It was a small gesture, but it spoke volumes about her state of mind. She was scared, but she was also trying to stay strong, to not let the fear control her. It made me admire her strength even more, but also heightened my resolve to protect her.

Whoever was after Aimee was prepared to go to any lengths to get her. The thought of her being in danger made my blood run cold.

He was Hannibal Lecter 2.0.

We needed to stop him before it was too late.

Twenty-Eight

Aimee

"Host will join shortly" flashed across the screen. I should have canceled this consultation session that Dr. Taitt arranged. The message continued to glare at me, reminding me of my reluctance. My fingers drummed nervously on the desk, and my knee bounced under the table. My mind wandered to Drago. The weight of this situation showed in every line that marred his handsome face yesterday. Except for breakfast at 8:00 a.m. and our late dinner around 9:30 p.m., we had hardly spoken.

When I approached him to take my case, all this was the farthest thing from my mind. Sitting behind Drago's desk, surrounded by the smell of polished wood and leather, I focused on the library that took up the wall opposite me. I ran my fingers over the cool glass desktop. Our reality now resembled something between *The Bourne Identity*, which sat at one end of his fiction shelf, and *Kiss the Girls* at the other. Someone was after me, but who?

And why?

The why was buried somewhere in their sick mind, a place I couldn't reach or understand. Drago mentioned that he and Bishop were following some leads. By today, he hoped to have a clearer idea about his theory. Physically, my body was in better shape since working out with Drago. Emotionally, I was adrift. Drawing in a shaky breath littered with trepidation, I waged war against unruly nerves and the iron ring tightening around my chest second by second.

"The host has joined the meeting." The robotic sound snapped me back to the present.

A woman with blonde hair streaked with gray smiled at me. Her eyes were kind, exuding a warmth that radiated through the screen. "Hello, Aimee. I'm Dr. Cynthia Hayes. But please call me Cynthia."

I wasn't ready for this. Not now. Definitely not today.

"Aimee? Aimee!"

"Sorry. Sorry. What were you saying?" I forced a smile. Even to my own ears my voice sounded distant.

Dr. Hayes began explaining her background as a Christian sex therapist. I didn't even know that was a thing. Her clients were primarily married couples who might be adjusting norms due to medical procedures or trauma. Also, she worked with single women who experienced trauma.

She went on in an easy relaxing tone, but the words jumbled in my mind. It became difficult to follow. "Dr. Hayes. I mean, Cynthia, I should have called to cancel."

She leaned back in her chair, her expression patient. "Want to share with me your thoughts on why you wanted to cancel?"

I hesitated, then took a deep breath. "Sex. Intimacy. Are the farthest thing from my thoughts. We're not even in the same room. More like different planets."

Pushing up her glasses on her nose, she leaned forward slightly. "Are you sure this isn't your mind trying to stall you from exploring this area? Talking about intimacy can be challenging."

My phone buzzed, startling me. It was a message from Drago. My heart raced as I read it. "Dr. Hayes, sorry. Bill me double the rate for this session." My eyes flicked back to the message. "I have to go."

Twenty-Nine

Drago

A nagging sensation lingered at the back of my mind. Something was missing. Aimee's focus on what happened in Paris channeled our efforts in that direction, but this person's fixation—better yet, obsession—with Aimee was personal. Being her first sexual experience in his twisted mind seemed to hold significant importance to him. He planned and strategized meticulously to ensure it happened. He must have been watching her long before Paris.

With these thoughts swirling in my head, I delved into Aimee's public life before her modeling career, to the Miss World pageant, and even her family background, although both her parents were deceased. There had to be clues buried in her past we hadn't yet uncovered.

After calling in some favors and paying for information from those who preferred not to owe anyone, I tracked down the woman who originally won the crown but stepped down after the scandal. She now ran a charity in honor of her sister, who was born with Down syndrome and had passed away three years ago. When I explained that Aimee's life was in danger, and that I believed the person might have been around even during her Miss World days, she agreed to speak with me this morning. I recorded the conversation, promising it would not go beyond us.

She was cautious and sent me an NDA while we were on the phone, which I reviewed, signed, and returned. Her revelations confirmed my suspicions. Although she was fluent in English, she occasionally slipped into Spanish when she became emotional.

I messaged Aimee, asking her to come down as soon as possible, emphasizing the importance. I also invited Jaden and Bishop. Bishop had already joined the conference call. I updated the whiteboard with all the information I gathered for discussion at the meeting. As Aimee entered, followed by Jaden, my eyes lingered on her. She walked with an upright posture, but the tightness around her eyes and the furrowed lines on her forehead reflected the turmoil racking her body.

Sliding into a chair, she said, "Good morning," probably more to Bishop, who filled the screen and wore his signature smile, which charmed many women into spilling secrets that helped us with investigations. His voice boomed a similar response.

I brought them up to speed with my theory and shared my whiteboard on the screen so Bishop could see as well. "I want us to process what I'm going to share." My attention focused on Aimee's face. "I think our sole focus on Paris was misplaced." Her eyes stayed on my face, wide with anticipation. "This started before. Paris was a major catalyst, but this was set in motion earlier."

"What?" Aimee asked, glancing at the screen. "You have the pageant on the board. Why?"

"It could have been a random person targeting you. But the messages sound personal." I didn't want to explain everything with Bishop and Jaden present. "Listen to this conversation from this morning." I pressed play.

"Sí, Señor Baas. Yes. You can record. I'll do anything to help Miss Aimee."

Aimee leaned forward, her eyes narrowing as Jaden opened his tablet and Valentina's voice filled the room. Valentina spoke steadily, almost detached, about how she never wanted to be in the pageant in the first place. Her father was wealthy and well-connected, driven by a need to prove something to the world after his first daughter was born with Down syndrome.

"*Mi hermana*, Elena, never lived." Valentina's voice wavered, and Aimee's breath hitched, her hand moving to her throat, fingers trembling slightly. Even her breathing seemed to still.

Valentina continued, describing how her father's shame for his oldest daughter twisted into an obsession, causing him to focus all his attention on Valentina. He needed the world to see that he had the most beautiful and accomplished daughter, going to any lengths—bribery, blackmail—to ensure her victory.

"When I bungled my question in the final," Valentina confessed, "I knew Aimee was going to win. I was absolutely shocked when they crowned me."

A long pause followed, heavy with unspoken memories. Valentina's voice softened, nearly breaking. "Two months into my reign, I was invited to an exclusive party. I can't even recall doing the drugs. Two days later, the pictures of me were all over the internet."

Aimee's jaw tightened, and she shifted slightly, her gaze hardening as the story continued to unfold.

"A week later, I received a note. 'I set the wrongs right. You cheated.' I knew then the entire thing was a setup. But the person was correct; my father did pay money. I should not have won. I was not all innocent, because I was old enough to stop. I was twenty-five at the time. But I started to love the attention."

Thirty

Aimee

"I set the wrongs right." The phrase ricocheted in my head. How long has this person been lurking and watching me? A shiver ran down my back, and goosebumps dotted my arms. My body remained in the chair, but my mind traveled to a safe place. God, tell me none of this is real. Let me wake up and find Topaz and me sitting around the table having breakfast, chatting about building our website for our villas.

None of this was real.

This was not real.

A voice.

A hand touched mine.

"Aimee. Aimee?"

My name whispered.

The reality I wanted to escape dragged me back, but I couldn't. Turning my head and blinking, I focused on the gold specks in his hazel eyes. My heart galloped as if it was at the Kentucky Derby.

"Aimee, tell me four things you can see in this room."

Gripping his hand, I said, "I can see you. I can see you."

"I want you to take a sip of the water Jaden placed on the table. Open it and sip."

Releasing his hand, I cracked the seal and sipped the water. I've fought to be strong, and in another life, I would not want to appear weak, especially surrounded by all men. *Pull yourself together. Don't let this creep win.*

Sitting straighter in the chair and letting out a breath, I focused on Drago. "Sorry."

"No need. We need to ask you some questions about your past."

Glancing at Bishop and Jaden, I said, "There's not much to tell."

Bishop smiled. Someone should capture Bishop's smile and post it on every billboard in New York City.

With his smile still in place, he said, "Our questions will guide you."

I nodded.

Bishop asked, "You moved to Etim when you were nine?"

"No. Ten. Dad got promoted to CEO of the company. The head office was here. He and Maa stayed until he retired, and they returned to Sri Lasara. I returned for a short time. But, I loved Etim."

Drago asked, "When you said you returned, how long was that?"

"Three months. I helped Maa plan the retirement party for Dad. The party was mainly former work colleagues and distant family members. Dad was an only child. Maa was Canadian; Dad introduced me to so many people, including his best friend, my godfather. He had a son who was not there. His wife was sick."

Closing my eyes, I conjured up Maa's sweet face—those soft gray eyes, slightly slanted, always filled with warmth and understanding. Her black curly hair framed her round cheeks perfectly, giving her a youthful glow even as she aged. I remember how her laughter could fill a room, the way her eyes would crinkle at the corners, making her look almost mischievous. Maa was the heart of our family.

"She died a year after Dad retired," I said, my voice trembling slightly as the memories flooded me. "It was so sudden—a massive stroke. I didn't get to tell her goodbye. She was the best."

They continued asking questions about life before the pageant, during, and after. They asked about people I met during high school and guys who invited me out. Many guys invited me out in high school, but I often said no, and my parents were strict about dating. I explained that my grandfather believed in arranged marriages, but Dad, although he said he would not do the same to me, didn't want me going boy crazy.

"Boy crazy?" Jaden asked.

"His words, not mine."

Thinking about my dad brought a smile to my face, a bittersweet warmth that spread through me. But it also unearthed something deeper, a memory I hadn't allowed myself to revisit in a long time. I leaned forward, my voice softening as I began to share. "Six months after the pageant, dad started calling me every week to check in. At first, I wondered if something was wrong—if he was sick, but didn't want to tell me. I couldn't shake the feeling that there was more behind those calls. Then, toward the end of my time as Miss World, he died in a car accident." My lips tried to curve upward, but the weight of the memory held them back. "He was a wonderful father. I never got to tell him how much I loved him."

Drago's eyes darkened, a silent exchange passing between him and Jaden.

"On it, boss," Jaden said, already moving into action.

Thirty-One

Drago

After questioning Aimee and speaking with Valentina yesterday, I'm certain of a couple of things. This began before Paris, and the person had deep pockets—very deep pockets—to orchestrate a coverup of this magnitude. The question on my mind, though, was why then, and why now?

With Aimee unable to leave without Jaden or me, Tanisha invited her over yesterday after our meeting to see her greenhouse and lab. That put a smile on her face. She missed her plants. Pushing open the door to my home office, I pointed downstairs, signaling I was leaving. She gave a small wave. Walking into my office for my 2:00 p.m. meeting, I found it difficult to get Aimee off my mind. I could see that the weight of the situation resided on her physically: her eyes held dark circles underneath them, and her shoulders which were usually model erect, were now hunched. Something ludicrous jumped into my mind. Peeking at my watch, I saw I had fifteen minutes to get my plans in place. I needed this as much as she did.

As I ended my call, Jaden came in and alerted me that the ambassador was parking. Powering on the screen, I saw that Bishop was already there. He asked, "How's your girl?"

His usual teasing was absent from his voice. I didn't want to deny it. She was my girl, but I wasn't ready to admit it out loud. There was something between us, but I didn't know if I should explore it.

"Literally hanging in there. I can see the strain. But she's rolling with each punch."

Bishop's expression softened. "Bro, we will get him."

I sighed. "All of these don't end like the movies. In the real world—"

"No," Bishop interrupted, his gaze steady. The intensity in his eyes gave off an unwavering reassurance. "That's why we're here."

"Going to meet the ambassador. We'll be back shortly."

Aimee

The penthouse, with its fortified walls and state-of-the-art security, was supposed to be impenetrable. Almost. Since the drone incident, the curtains remained drawn, casting the room in a perpetual twilight, only thin slivers of daylight managing to sneak through the cracks. I stood by one of those narrow openings, peering out at the world beyond—the sprawling Etim skyline, once a symbol of freedom, now a reminder of my confinement. A month ago, I walked those streets without a second thought, the shadows of Paris lingering in my mind but never fully imprisoning me. Now, a different kind of shadow kept me prisoner—a monster lurking in the dark, biding his time, while I was the one trapped. The irony wasn't lost on me. The more I sought to get free, the more the locks clicked into place. All for my protection from this unknown psycho.

A gentle brush against my leg brought me back to the present, the soft, familiar feel of Sebastian's tail as he wound around me. I bent down and scooped him into my arms. "Hi, big boy. Drago will be home soon, and we'll eat," I cooed, finding a small measure of comfort in the way he rubbed his head against me, purring softly.

The sound of the lift opening broke the quiet tension in the room. Drago stepped out, his strong presence filling the space as he sauntered in with a takeout bag in his hand. I offered earlier to warm up something Stacey left, but even that simple task seemed too much to bear today.

Sebastian's ears perked up, his attention fully on Drago now. I set him down gently and went to wash my hands, then took the food from Drago as he handed it to me. "How was your day?" I asked, trying to infuse some normalcy into my voice to keep the conversation light.

"Hoping it made yours better," he replied, his gaze softening as it met mine, something unspoken lingered in his eyes.

I furrowed my brow, tilting my head in confusion. What did he mean?

"Give me ten minutes. I got Thai. Set out the food. I'm going to change," he said, his voice carrying a hint of anticipation.

I busied myself with setting the table, Sebastian already attacking his own meal. But Drago's words stayed with me, swirling in my mind.

Make my day better? What could he have done? I set out the dishes while the question simmered in my mind. Drago walked back into the room, hair still damp from the shower, a white T-shirt clung to his frame and black joggers hung just right—honestly, those should be illegal. The corners of his mouth twitched, as if they held back a smile he couldn't quite contain.

"Come and eat, and tell me how you made my day better," I urged, my curiosity now fully piqued.

He sat beside me, his presence warm and solid, anchoring me in the moment. "There's one condition," he said, his tone light but with a hint of mischief.

"What's the condition?" I asked, lifting my fork, a smile tugging at my lips despite myself.

His grin broke free, broad and genuine. "You can't say no."

My smile matched his now, the weight of the day lifting just a little. "Okay. Yes," I agreed, wondering what on earth he had planned.

Thirty-Two

Aimee

"I'm going to die!" I screamed. Drago laughed as the roller coaster took its final loop. The wind rushed against my face and my heart galloped. I never thought hanging upside down for the entire ride was my thing. But the ride kept its promise, placing a smile on my face. No wonder they call the roller coaster "Smiler."

As the ride stopped, my heart slowed to a trot. Drago's smile took up his whole face, like a kid excited about their first trip to the zoo. Taking my hand, he helped me out of the roller coaster. Our hands remained linked as we walked toward the exit, after stopping to purchase the picture that was taken of us on the ride. My eyes were closed, and my mouth was opened; on closer inspection, I'm certain you would have been able to see my tonsils. Peering up at him as we strolled past people scrambling to get to their last ride before the park closed, I said, "This was not what I expected when I said yes. But Alton Towers was what I needed."

"Our magical time is not over. You, Cinderella, don't change at midnight. I have an entire night and morning planned before we return home."

Taking a deep breath, I inhaled the crisp air as we walked to meet our driver. The passing country scenery of tall, majestic trees was stunning. Despite the numerous times I traveled to England, my trips kept me in London. Squeezing Drago's hand, I said, "Thank you."

After fifteen minutes of driving, we pulled up to what resembled a large country estate, the kind you would see in a historical romance movie. The driver took our carry-on bags, and a butler greeted us. A real butler. Not even Shae's sister Sapphire, with all her wealth—she was wealthier than Shae—had a butler, with the black tailcoat and all.

As we approached, the butler nodded and, with the most polished British accent I've ever heard in person, said, "Good afternoon, Mr. Baas, Ms. Patel. Welcome to Hartwell Manor. My name is Peter, and I am here to ensure your stay is both comfortable and memorable. May I assist you with your luggage and show you to your suite?"

"Thank you," Drago replied.

Peter looked up at Drago. "Everything has been arranged to your request."

Walking into the suite, which was a little larger than the guest bedroom I stayed in at Drago's, I saw that it opened to a garden.

My throat tightened, and my eyes stung. I was moved by the thoughtfulness of him booking this room because he knew my love for plants. Even at this time of day, it was still possible to see the reds and yellows. Opening the door, I rushed outside and stood, soaking it in for a few minutes. Without turning, I felt the dizzying effects of Drago's masculinity. Drago didn't scare me. I welcomed him. On some level, I craved him. He stood behind me and wrapped me in his arms, resting his chin on my head.

I said, "This is breathtaking."

Placing a kiss on my head, he said, "Come. We have thirty minutes to get ready. We're sharing a room. You get the bed. I will take the pull-out sofa in the sitting area. I feel much safer this way. Go and get ready."

Staying in a room with a man should have sent off warning bells. Not with Drago. If he wanted to do something, he could have done so in the five weeks we'd been together. But he has always been the perfect gentleman. Maybe too perfect. I've seen the times his eyes dropped to my lips. If only I was brave enough...

Once in the bathroom, I paired black jeans with a gray cashmere sweater. Stepping back to check the fit, I was shocked to realize the woman staring at me from the mirror looked a little like me before the first message. A warm glow brightened my cheeks. Tidying the counter so Drago could have some space, I opened the door and said, "All yours."

He turned and made a sharp intake on seeing me. "I pray when I'm finished, I look at least half as good as you."

Smiling, I said, "There is a magic mirror in there. When you look in it, it does wonders for your self-esteem."

He laughed, and I went onto the patio to watch people stroll the gardens. Couples sat on benches. The air carried the honey scent of the sweet pea flowers. Tomorrow, I'm going to take pictures for Tanisha. She would absolutely appreciate this garden.

Drago cleared his throat in a very theatrical manner.

"Are you trying to get my attention, sir?"

"Sir. Very British, are we now?" Drago asked with a smile playing on his lip. "My lady, will you join me for dinner?"

"How could I even think of turning down such a dashing man?"

Extending his hand to me, he said, "Instead of modeling, maybe we should get you a spot on Broadway."

Rounding the sofa, I saw food set out picnic style on a thick carpet. Candles glowed on the table, which held a wine bucket and glasses.

"Drago, my goodness."

"Let's sit."

Dinner was roasted lamb served with red potatoes and vegetables. After we ate, we rested our backs against the sofa. I licked my spoon as I finished my sticky toffee pudding.

"I can't move. I might have to unbutton my jeans. That food was so good."

Drago cleared the plates and stacked them on the cart, rolling it outside the room. Returning to sit beside me, he poured himself a glass of wine. Taking a sip, he glanced at me.

Resting my hand on his, I said, "This entire day was lovely."

He drew me close to him, and I snuggled against him and watched as the flames of the candle flickered and the light faded outside. *Be brave, Aimee.* Drago set his glass down.

One...only one. A tiny one. You can do it.

Drago turned his head toward me. I leaned in and grazed my lips over his. He inhaled and pulled me toward him, his tongue invading my mouth.

The sticky toffee tasted better on his tongue than on my spoon.

Thirty-Three

Drago

Nothing in my dreams compared to this moment. A soft moan escaped her, and I shifted, lifting her onto my lap without breaking contact. Aimee wrapped her hands around my neck, and I rested my hand on her waist to keep her from moving. If she ground against me, I would definitely embarrass myself, thirty-nine or not.

Pulling away, I trailed kisses along the side of her neck. God, help me keep my hands in check. Every fiber of my being screamed to push my hand under her sweater, to feel the warmth of her skin against my palm, but I knew one touch would shatter my restraint. Aimee ran her fingers through my hair, leaned forward, and followed my lead, running her tongue over my neck.

Any ideas I had to restrain her movement did not work. My hands sat on her waist as she so very gently circled her hips against me. I was going to...

Everything tingled.

"Drago..." she breathed.

I wanted to unbutton and pull down her pants and rid that sweater from between us so I could place her on the rug and worship her body. Instead, I said, "You, Miss Aimee Patel, will be my undoing. Come on before I lose all self-control."

She leaned and placed gentle kisses along my jawline, lifting her gray eyes toward me. "The great Drago Baas, losing his self-control?"

She tested her theory by undoing another button. With the top two already open, she had easy access to my chest. She leaned in, her tongue tracing a tantalizing path over my skin, deliberately avoiding my nipple, which only made the ache for her touch more unbearable. If she did, I would be done. But before this escalated further...

"Come, my lady. Before this scoundrel ravages you. Plus, we still have plans in the morning before we go home tomorrow."

We both stood up, our hands still linked. She tilted her head and peered up at me with pupils wide and intense, a stark contrast against her silver irises. Running her tongue over her bottom lip, she asked, "Who says I don't want to be ravaged by a scoundrel?"

Thirty-Four

Drago

The elevator doors slid open, and the weight I left behind Saturday morning settled on my shoulders again. Sebastian was pacing back and forth, clearly impatient to see his favorite person. Aimee bent over and stroked his fur. "Big boy, were you good to Stacey?"

As Aimee gave Sebastian his much-needed attention, the cat gave me his back and lifted his tail, showing me his ample rear. I shook my head. The damn cat was totally bewitched by Aimee. Can't blame him.

Straightening, Aimee tiptoed and placed a kiss on my cheek. "Thanks for the weekend." Her cheeks flushed as she smiled. "And for being the perfect gentleman. It was a wonderful experience. Can't wait to show Tanisha the pictures."

Holding onto her, I rubbed my cheek against hers and nibbled her earlobe. "Go, before I forget how to be the perfect gentleman. My back is looking forward to making a connection with my bed and not a sofa."

"Your fault. I could have taken the sofa. But that bed was lovely. Nowhere near the Anson Resort."

She went to her room to change before visiting Tanisha. The moment she left, an emptiness filled the space she had occupied. Walking into my bedroom, my large custom-made bed never looked so wonderful. Moving to the sitting area in the corner of the room, I checked the emails Jaden and Bishop had sent. Jaden reported that no information on Aimee's father's car accident could be found. As occurred in Paris, someone wiped everything clean.

Bishop arranged a conference call for tomorrow to update us on the ambassador's case. Jaden said he would continue looking, but I knew he would find nothing. Leaning back, I pinched the bridge of my nose. All these dead ends. Eventually, he will slip, and we'll be there to catch him. Anything else would be unthinkable.

When I closed my eyes, last night replayed behind my lids like a 3-D movie. It took everything not to follow her into her room and take things a little further...or much further. Before even going there, I want to be certain of my feelings. This was certainly more than lust. Her very essence seeped into me. The last time I experienced anything like this was the day I walked into class and my eyes landed on Minerva. Getting up, I walked to the bar, which was part of the sitting area, and poured myself a glass of Yamazaki 18-Year-Old. A client gifted me a bottle of this whiskey two years ago, and ever since, I'd always kept a bottle in stock. I loved the balance. It carried notes of dark chocolate and dried fruit, with a hint of spice.

Sipping my drink, I walked to the floor-to-ceiling window, opened the drapes, and looked out at the skyline.

Bishop came on screen, his characteristic smile absent. "Jaden joining us?"

"No. He's gone with Aimee. She needed to go home to meet with Leila. Also, Tanisha wanted to see her greenhouse. They've bonded over plants."

"I hope for your sake that's all they bonded over."

A smiled tugged at my lips due to his comment.

Bishop informed me that the leak in the Ambassador's office was coming from his deputy. He was plotting to bring him down with an international scandal. We agreed he would forward the report after I reviewed it.

Getting up from my chair, I walked over and stood in front of the screen. Arching a brow, I asked, "Want to tell me what's going on?"

"Nothing—"

"We've been together too long. Don't give me that crap."

His Adam's apple bobbed up and down. He clenched his jaw. "I met someone."

"And?"

A laugh spilled out from him, more potent than a triple shot of espresso.

"The next time you were in Miami, I planned on introducing you to her. That will never happen."

She died? I didn't want to voice my thoughts.

"You will never meet her because the last time I saw her, she was in bed, literally sleeping her way to the top with her boss."

Thirty-Five

Aimee

When the helicopter landed, I saw my vehicle. Chef Andre had promised to make the arrangements. We all got out of the chopper, including Leila, who met us in the city for the ride over. Tanisha pointed to the construction. "This is crazy."

My face warmed. Taking in the sprawling site reminded me of what Topaz fought for and accomplished. "It's something, isn't it?"

"Jaden, when this place opens, for the craziness and sleepless nights you put me through, I want a weekend. No! An entire week."

"Some suites will have private pools."

"Taking notes, Jaden?" Tanisha asked.

Bending, he kissed her on the head. "Only one week?"

The chopper waited, as our visit was to last no longer than one hour. Since Topaz got Mark to place the deliveries for me in my office, I had not returned to check these accessories or enter them in the system. Once that was done, Leila could sort out the shipment of the accessories to the manufacturers.

"Aimee, hand me your keys. Remain in the vehicle while I check both places," Jaden instructed.

Tanisha leaned forward. "Out here is so beautiful. I can hear the distant crashing of the waves. Some place to visit. A good getaway. But I could not see myself living here in Needhams. I love the city, with all the activity in Marigot."

"I'm with you there," Leila added.

"Until staying with Drago, I never understood the attraction of the city. But I still see Needhams as home."

Jaden checked the duplex and gave the all clear for us to get out of the vehicle. As we went in, Jaden's eyes scanned the surroundings. I left my bag in the vehicle but took my phone.

I showed Tanisha the greenhouse then Leila and I went to the office and worked on the accessories. Within thirty minutes, we were through the boxes, and I left Leila to input the items into the system. While I was here, I planned to grab some more clothes before joining Tanisha and giving her a proper tour of the greenhouse.

Rushing up the stairs, I picked up and packed a few items. On my way down, my eyes connected with the orchid. My gosh, the orchid Topaz sent! I had forgotten all about it. I touched the drooping leaves and then took it outside.

Approaching the greenhouse, I spotted Tanisha's head first, her crown braid perfectly framing her face. She always kept her hair up, which was practical, given the work she did. As I stepped inside, she glanced up at me, her eyes wide with excitement. "This place is so chill. I love the vibe. And you've been holding out on me. You have not one, but *two* Rothschild's Slipper Orchids."

Those orchids were more than just rare—they were nearly impossible to find. Their delicate beauty and the patience required to care for them always resonated with me. A quiet challenge amid the chaos of my life. "They're special."

I took in her smiling face; I knew she would love it. "When we next have a chance, I'll let you take a piece of the plant."

"Oh my gosh, really? That would be great. Thanks." Studying the item in my hand, she added, "That pot is beautiful." Her nose wrinkled. "Can't say the same for the plant."

"I know. I forgot it with everything that's going on."

She took it from me. "Let's see what little love we can give it before we head out."

Leila came and informed us that she was all done. Returning to the house, I picked up the carry-on and my phone. As I walked out to the vehicle, the phone vibrated in my hand. I glanced at it and saw that the message was from an unknown number. I did not answer; nothing was going to destroy this peace.

As the messages kept coming, the phone continued hissing like a snake. Just like the sender.

Thirty-Six

Drago

Jaden messaged when they were on their way back to the chopper, mentioning that Aimee's phone was blowing up with messages, which she refused to answer. The unease brewing inside me intensified as I pulled up the report from the tracking application I installed on her phone and scanned the locations. My jaw tightened as I read the list, and my body tensed in response. Sweat beaded on my forehead as a cold, relentless dread seeped into my bones.

Anson Island Resort. Alton Towers. Hartwell Manor. Needhams.

He was taunting us. Challenging us.

Aimee, in her brave attempt to maintain a facade of normalcy, invited everyone to Vibrant Bowls for an early dinner. My mind raced, playing out one dark scenario after another, each one more troubling than the last. Every second she spent outside these walls made my skin crawl. I needed her back within the sanctuary of the penthouse, where I could ensure her safety. The thought of her out in the open, exposed, gnawed at me, twisting my gut until it was a tight knot of anxiety.

Grabbing the key fob for the Range Rover, I was out the door in seconds, my strides long and urgent as I headed to join them. This wasn't a game—it was a battle of wills, a fight for control, and I refused to let him win.

He was close.

He wanted us to know.

But he underestimated how far I was willing to go to protect what was mine.

Thirty-Seven

Aimee

Read.

Don't Read.

These words bounced around my head as if Roger Federer and Rafeal Nadal was playing a match, and my head was center court. I did everything to avoid reading these messages. But deep down, I knew I needed to read them. I clicked on the icon.

My eyes connected with the first message. My hands trembled as message after messaged filled the screen.

Unknown

Aimee. I'm coming for you.

I hope I'm still the only man that ever touched you like that.

You're MINE.

Why do you let things I give you die?

You did not take good care of my gift. You left it to die. Weeks you did not come home.

Weeks.

I should punish you.

Disappointed.

I gave you a gift five years ago. A part of me. You let it die too.

"Oh, God. No. No." The sound of something crashing filled the air as my legs buckled beneath me. I slid to the floor, my back hitting the bed, unable to hold myself upright any longer.

I was disappointed when the doctor gave me the news. How could you?

I will remedy that soon. You're MINE. My family. My soon-to-be wife.

The phone slipped from my hand, clattering to the floor as if the very device betrayed me. My chest tightened, and my breath caught in my throat as I curled into myself, tucking my knees into my chest, seeking the smallest possible space in this room that somehow dropped at least ten degrees in temperature. No matter how tightly I wrapped my arms around my legs, the cold seeped into my bones. My body trembled uncontrollably, every muscle taut and shivering.

A shadow fell over me. I squeezed my eyes shut, the darkness behind my lids safer than whatever loomed above. Panic surged, erupting from deep within me.

"Don't touch me!

Don't touch me!

Don't touch me!"

The words tore from my throat, desperate and raw, a frantic plea to keep the nightmare at bay.

"Aimee, it's me." The voice came from somewhere distant, distorted by the fog of terror that clouded my mind.

"No! Don't. Touch. Me."

Thirty-Eight

Drago

The faint crash echoed through the room, freezing something deep within me, yet my body sprang into action, moving with lightning speed toward the bedroom where Aimee stayed.

I had fooled myself.

Shaking my head, I was certain he could not reach her behind these walls. My home should have been safe for Aimee. But once he was out there, she would never be safe.

For five minutes she screamed, "Don't touch me." Not even Minerva's death made me so powerless. I called Dr. Taitt and asked her to come. I think I more demanded than asked. Watching the woman I love, I rested my head against the cool glass. The realization that I loved Aimee washed over me like a tidal wave: overwhelming and undeniable.

Dr. Taitt promised to get her phone opened, so we could see the messages, this sick—

The click-clack of feet moved in my direction. Turning, Dr. Taitt extended the phone to me, her expression grave. She exhaled. “You should not get emotionally attached to patients. But I’ve seen Aimee struggle to put this behind her.” Shaking her head, she added, “Now, she’s ready to move forward, and this monster wants to destroy her.”

Taking the phone from her, I locked eyes with Dr. Taitt, as she said, “There is nothing that can prepare you for what you will read, no matter how much psychology training you have.” Her throat bobbed up and down. “I’ve been practicing for over twenty years. I’ve seen all kinds of things. But not this.”

Her words hung heavy in the air, a grim precursor to the actual messages themselves. With each word I read, my grip on the phone increased. “If this is true, the doctor was part of this entire coverup.”

Sitting to process this message, the weight of it crushed me. No wonder she doesn’t want anyone to touch her.

“Topaz is her next of kin, and I called her.”

“Why? Why did you call her?”

“Aimee wants to leave.”

“She can’t leave. There’s a sociopath out there. Here, he can’t physically get to her, and I am not going to allow her to look at any more of these messages without someone present.”

“You know, she needs to process all of this.”

I looked at my pristine floor. "I love her." My voice was tight and guttural.

Dr. Taitt touched my hand. "She will need it. I'm going to take her to my retreat center. The security is top-notch."

Conflicted, I struggled between my need to protect her and my understanding of her need for professional help. Dr. Taitt gave me a gentle squeeze as the click-clack of her heels carried back up the stairs. Sebastian sat outside the door, vigilant. Moments later, Dr. Taitt returned with Aimee. Her head was tipped down; her hair shielded her face.

Grabbing my keys, I waited until I knew they were out of the building and followed. Ensuring their safety was paramount.

After following them for about thirty minutes, I saw the vehicle turn into the retreat center. The gate closed between us as Dr. Taitt helped Aimee out of the vehicle.

I did two things that I have not done in five years. Leaning over on the steering wheel, the first fat tear dropped from my eye...

And I prayed.

Thirty-Nine

Drago

The irregular thud in my chest quickened, then slowed. My heart beat without rhythm. Silence pressed against my ears in the penthouse, the buildup making them pop. Passing Aimee's room this morning, I saw Sebastian curled up on her pillow. I stomped into the office at 5:35 a.m., my knuckles raw and red from an hour of pummeling the punching bag.

The scent of fresh coffee filled the conference room as Jaden entered. My jacket hung on the chair where Aimee had sat during her first visit, the memory cascading over me like a comforting breeze. Jaden's hand clapped my shoulder, before he settled with his own steaming cup. Bishop's face flickered to life on the screen moments later, the bags under his eyes betraying a sleepless night.

"Bro. We'll nail this psycho," Bishop growled, his jaw clenching around the words.

I rolled up my sleeves, the whiteboard before me a maze of connections. My fingers twitched, itching to draw the lines only I could see. "Sri Lasara. That's where this started."

Bishop's brow arched. "What's your reasoning?"

"This psycho knew Aimee pre-Paris. Deep pockets. Well-connected. Two elaborate parties—the one with Valentina and the one where he got the fashion house to host a private showing for him. That was all child's play for him. And those messages...they reek of entitlement. Like Aimee was some birthright." The words tasted bitter in my mouth.

Jaden leaned in, his chair creaking. "So why go dark for so long?"

"Maybe life got in the way," Bishop mused, fingers drumming on his desk.

"Prison?" Jaden suggested.

Bishop scoffed. "With that kind of cash? Not a chance. Political aspirations, perhaps?"

"Since when has that stopped anyone?" Jaden retorted, his jacket falling open.

"Family." The word hung in the air as I faced them, the weight of it pressing down on us all. "He called Aimee his family. Wants to marry her. What if he had a family before, but lost them? A recent change?"

Jaden and Bishop straightened, energy crackling between us. "We narrow the pool," I said, my voice low and intense. "Wealthy. Connected to Aimee's father, if not her directly. And a personal loss in the last year."

The pieces clicked into place, each connection sparking through my nerves. A chill raced down my spine as the implications unfolded, the enormity of our discovery threatening to suffocate me.

Pushing back his chair, Jaden's eyes gleamed with determination. "I'm heading to Sri Lasara. I think I'll take Tanisha with me."

Bishop, ever the pragmatist, but not missing an opportunity to tease Jaden, said, "No dead bodies, unless you find this psycho." With those parting words, the screen went dark, and I was alone.

My gaze drifted to the picture of Aimee and me on the Smiler at Alton Towers. *We're getting there.*

Soon, Aimee.

Soon.

Glancing at the board, I made a circle on it. "You're mine. I'm coming to get you."

Forty

Aimee

The cool morning air caressed my skin as I turned my face to the early sun. "You need a little more fertilizer, and you'll be good as new in a few days," I whispered to the struggling plant. The garden's tranquility contrasted sharply with the chaos in my mind. Sticking the fork into the soil and sitting, I reflected on the past three days. Home wasn't an option. Going to Drago wasn't one, either. The thought of him sent shock waves of sadness throughout my system.

The vibrant flowers around me seemed to mock my inner turmoil. A butterfly landed on a pink hibiscus, its delicate wings fluttering in the breeze before it took flight. The sight stirred a deep longing within me—freedom, so close yet so far.

Dr. Taitt and I spoke yesterday for the first time. The madness of this situation defied comprehension. How had my life spiraled to this point? The monster pursuing me, the secrets unraveling...it all seemed like a nightmare I couldn't wake from.

Footsteps crunched on the gravel path, disturbing my sanctuary. Thoughts about where I would go next swirled in my mind. A tomorrow problem, certainly, but one that loomed large.

"Aimee."

Topaz's voice broke through my reverie. I rushed into her arms, the dam holding back my emotions finally breaking. Everything poured out at once—fear, confusion, relief.

"Do you want to go in or remain out here?" Topaz asked, her voice gentle.

"Out here," I replied, breathing in the scent of flowers and earth. "Dr. Taitt shouldn't have called you. You have enough on your plate."

We returned to the bench. Resting my head on her shoulder, we listened to the birds chirping, the morning peace wrapping around us like a comforting blanket.

"I was—"

"You don't have to talk about it."

Shaking my head, I steeled myself. "I need to. With you."

Her gaze remained steady, a silent question in her eyes. "He or she would have been five by now." The weight of unspoken words hung between us. "Is it wrong that a part of me feels relieved? Does that make me a bad person?"

Squeezing her hand, I drew strength from her non-judgmental presence. "Am I a bad person?"

"Oh, Aimee. You are human. You are sweet, loving, and kind."

The sun rose further in the sky, its warmth growing more intense. "Let's go in."

"If you're worrying about my skin, baby hormones have not been good to me. A little sun is the least of my acne's problems."

"You're beautiful all the time," I told her, meaning every word.

We walked to the retreat restaurant, the transition from the lush garden to the airy interior jarring. Floor-to-ceiling windows framed the view of the garden we'd just left. We ordered breakfast: two egg-white omelets with multigrain toast and a pot of decaffeinated coffee.

"Where's Shae?"

Topaz explained that he'd set up meetings with the construction team; they planned on returning to Miami that evening. We ate breakfast in silence, the clink of cutlery punctuating our thoughts.

Pouring myself a cup of coffee, I said, "Something should have clicked that you would not have sent me that orchid."

"Me sending a plant is definitely a no-no."

"I don't know how much you were told."

As people came and went around us, we remained seated, our conversation a lifeline in the sea of uncertainty I found myself in. Talking to Topaz, as always, brought a sense of relief. I'd made so much progress since Drago came into my life. But a nagging question persisted. How does he see me? I don't even know how I see myself.

My mouth twitched into a smile, a memory surfacing.

"What placed that smile on your lips?"

"I told you about Alton Towers. I kissed Drago. Like a real kiss, not just a peck on the cheek."

"And?"

The memory of his lips on mine sent warmth spreading across my face.

"You're blushing." Topaz teased.

"Shush."

Pulling my hair over my shoulder, I shared the question that had been screaming in my head. "Would he want me? He knows. He knows everything."

Topaz reached across the table and gave my hand a gentle squeeze. Her phone vibrated. She released my hand and shifted her gaze from the phone. "Shae is now leaving the site. Do you want to come to Miami?"

I shook my head, though a part of me yearned to say yes. But running away wasn't the option. This monster wasn't going away. Wherever I went, he would follow. The realization sent a chill through me, despite the warmth of the restaurant.

I was certain he knew I was here.

Forty-One

Drago

Living along the beach on a Caribbean island can give one a false sense of security. That's how I ended up sitting in this villa, waiting for the owner to return. In less than thirty seconds, I picked the lock. They did not arm the security system when they left. The sun set outside, casting long shadows across the room. The scent of saltwater mingled with the tropical flora, creating a serene backdrop that belied the tension within.

Two hours crawled by, each minute stretching like elastic. My mind raced through scenarios, replaying Aimee's haunted expression when she spoke of her past. The weight of my gun pressed against my side. As darkness fell, it brought me closer to the impending confrontation.

Finally, movement. The spy camera I placed outside revealed a solitary figure. The person entered, setting down reusable shopping bags and packing away groceries. Such care for the environment, such disregard for human life. The irony twisted in my gut like a knife.

The villa's opulence mocked me. High ceilings and large windows let in the fading light, casting an orange glow on polished floors. The large island in the kitchen doubled as a breakfast bar, and right on the beach off the patio, an infinity pool ran the full length of the villa. Crime truly pays.

In the converted home office, head shots of young women littered the desk. A pile carried a sticky note with the word INTERESTED and the other had NO written on it, both notes in all caps. My jaw clenched. If they still worked in the field, that was about to end.

My target entered the bedroom and flipped the switch. The shock was written all over their face. As she turned to bolt, I spoke, my voice low and controlled despite the rage simmering beneath. "I wouldn't suggest that unless you want to end up behind bars. You have at least another twenty years before the statute of limitations expires."

"Get out now, before I call the gendarmes!" Her heavy French accent punctuated her speech.

"Yes, let's call the police. We can tell them how you were involved in a crime involving the former Miss World, Aimee Patel."

Her hand fell away from the door. The corners of her mouth trembled, struggling to form words, while her lips pressed tightly together, turning white. Her brow furrowed deeply, and she mumbled, "He sent you?... You're him?... We had a deal."

"Come in, Ms. Valmont. Have a seat. I don't bite." At least not yet. The thought of her living this idyllic life while Aimee battled with the demons of her past made my blood boil.

"Listen. I kept my part of the deal. I took the money and ran."

"You're going to sit on the bed and put your hands behind your back." My voice remained steady, but inside, a storm brewed.

"Didn't you hear me?" Her eyes darted around the room, frantic. "I kept my mouth shut!"

She attempted to bolt, but I moved swiftly, tackling her to the ground and cuffing her. Lifting her, I placed her on the queen-sized four-poster bed draped with a mosquito net.

Glaring at me, she spat, "Is this necessary? Dr. Dolos wanted to confess, and you got to her before she spoke to anyone. Why now? After all this time?"

It became obvious that she did not know the madman behind this elaborate plot, and she thought I was him. Jaden's message flashed in my mind—he'd narrowed the pool of suspects and would fly home tomorrow. With his information and what I'd extract from Ms. Valmont, we'd close in on this psycho.

A slow, deliberate satisfaction curled my lips, a dark pleasure spread through my chest. I rested my Heckler & Koch alongside my cell on the dresser opposite the bed. "I want to know everything about Aimee Patel and what you did to her, and why."

Her eyes widened further; her lips parted in a gasp. Sweat beaded on her forehead despite the cool evening. The blood drained from her face. "You're not him?"

Pieces fell into place. My heart raced with the thrill of the hunt, but I kept my voice steady. "No, Ms. Valmont. I'm much worse. Now, let's start from the beginning, shall we?"

Forty-Two

Drago

"I can't believe this is happening. This is absurd. *Vous êtes fou*!"

"You're correct. I'm crazy. And, I don't have all day. Talk."

Her once perfectly styled brunette hair was now scattered in all directions. Her chest rose and fell rapidly, each breath coming in quick, shallow bursts.

"The sooner you start, the sooner this will be all over."

Her eyes, accentuated by dramatic winged eyeliner, narrowed into piercing slits, fixed on me with an intensity that could cut through steel. "Promise?"

"Talk. Or should I say *parler*?" I said, returning to the chair. Being near her might be too much of a temptation. I'd never killed a woman, and I didn't plan on starting now. Her fate would be much worse.

"My fashion house was profitable, but we had cash flow issues. Therefore, we were having challenges securing some of the top models." She paused, closing her eyes before continuing. "The season was approaching and many of the top models were already making contracts. Aimee was new. The fresh face, and I wanted her. Sometimes, everything you want—what do they say? — is not always good for you."

I signaled her with a slight nod to continue.

"She received many offers. The highest was two million, but I wanted her. It was no secret. I received a call, offering to give me twelve million. Five million was to secure Aimee, including everything she would require for the contract period. The balance gave me the needed cash flow." She swallowed hard. "Once she was hired, the demands came."

"Like what?"

"He had a fixation on Aimee. They suggested I recommend vitamins to her since she was new to the industry."

Her head shook slightly, as if trying to dislodge the memory.

"Continue."

"They were hormone pills. Fertility medication from Dr. Dolos."

"Whose idea was this?"

"His, obviously."

A sour taste crept up my throat. The thought of someone knowingly giving her fertility medication disguised as vitamins turned my stomach.

"She was on the pills for three months before he asked for the private showing. Again, another five million went into the account, out of which all the models were paid, but Aimee received one million dollars, as she was to be the star of the show."

The weight of her words hung heavy in the air. My mind raced with the implications, the betrayal, and the sheer audacity of it all. I clenched my fists, every muscle in my body tense with controlled anger.

"Did you know his plans?"

She nodded.

"You were okay with some person drugging and taking advantage of another woman."

"From the start, his plan was always to get her pregnant. When he heard about the miscarriage, he threatened Dr. Dolos. She was scared and wanted to go to the police. She never made it."

She shook her head. "We controlled the clinic Aimee visited. Dr. Dolos was never on their payroll. Again, money was paid to make all of this happen."

Rising from the chair, I picked up my gun and paused the recording on my phone.

"You can't leave me like this."

A dark sense of pleasure twisted my mouth into a grin. "Don't worry. You won't be like that for long."

Forty-Three

Aimee

Walking into Dr. Taitt's office, I spotted a gift bag resting on the table next to her chair. Her eyes tracked my movement until I took a seat. My fingers tapped an erratic rhythm on the armrest, betraying the restlessness that plagued me.

She sat adjacent to me, the weight of her gaze resting on me. Her office, more like a sitting room you would find in a country manor like Hartwell, but on a smaller scale, held no formal desk. The chairs were upholstered in soft, buttery leather, inviting and comfortable. Sunlight streamed through the tall windows, casting warm, golden patches on the wooden floor. The faint scent of lavender lingered in the air, soothing yet invigorating.

No degrees littered her walls. Instead, bold abstract paintings adorned them. I often wondered if there was a psychological assessment behind the choices and not mere decoration. Her polished persona—hair permed and worn in a neat bun; always dressed in a skirt suit, either from Ann Taylor or Tahari's collection. There were a few pieces in my recent collection that would complement her curvy figure.

"Did you rest well last night?" she asked.

I stifled a yawn, my eyelids heavy. "The dreams came again. I eventually took the medication."

She nodded. "That's why I prescribed it. Have you given any thought to your next steps? You've been here a full week." Pushing up her glasses on her nose, her dark eyes remained focused on me as she continued, "You don't have to decide now, but you are free to go anytime. We can have weekly sessions, either in person or via conference call."

Go where? My gaze drifted to the window, the world outside suddenly vast and intimidating. We discussed this last week, but no clear path emerged. Miami was an option, but Topaz would be back in a week. Staying with them would bring trouble to their door. I pulled my hair over my shoulder, twisting it around my fingers. So many, many options, yet none were really options.

Settling my eyes on her and letting out a breath, I said, "I will decide in a few days."

Taking up the bag that rested beside her, she turned and handed it to me. "This is from Drago."

Drago?

He wanted to visit, but Dr. Taitt told him I would reach out when I was ready. My hands trembled as I reached for the bag, pulling out a new phone. There was a note:

There are so many things I want to tell you.

But right now, I want you to get better and know that Sebastian and I miss you.

This phone is safe. A digital tracker was on your last phone. That was how he knew all your locations.

Take care of yourself.

Drago

My breath caught in my throat as I read the words. The wallpaper showed Drago's beautiful hazel eyes twinkling back at me from the photo of us on the rollercoaster. The Smiler still brought a smile to my face. Warmth spread through my chest.

"Aimee, part of moving on is not only stopping this very sick person, but also being able to have a life. A relationship. Do you still want that?"

My eyes dropped and connected with Drago's. I let my finger trace his face on the screen, the cool glass a poor substitute for his warm skin. A lump formed in my throat, making it hard to swallow. Lifting my eyes to hers, I said, my voice barely above a whisper, "Yes. More than anything, I want that."

Forty-Four

Drago

The arrest of Lazelle Valmont would make the news, but the reason would remain hidden. This would make the evil mind behind this entire operation panic. Whatever he was planning, he would obviously fast-track. I hoped this pushed him to make a critical error.

This cat-and-mouse game needed to end. I was ready to end it.

My plane sat poised on the tarmac at Pointe-à-Pitre International Airport. The captain's voice crackled over the intercom, announcing our 11:00 p.m. takeoff. A glance at my watch showed fifteen minutes remaining. Etim was five hours ahead of Guadeloupe. Dr. Taitt was used to my untimely calls by now. With everything unfolding, Aimee's safety was a priority. I picked up the cell and dialed her number.

The phone rang twice before Dr. Taitt answered, her voice sharp, exasperated. “Drago Baas, you’re making this a habit.”

“Sorry for disturbing your sleep.”

“You don’t sound sorry one ounce,” she said, muffling a yawn.

“I need you to increase your security at the retreat facility. At least for the next few days.”

“Why?”

I exhaled slowly, my breath fogging the cool window beside me. “We’ve put some things into play, hoping to flush out this psycho.”

He killed Dr. Dolos. He would kill again. Would he make a play to silence Ms. Valmont? But she did not know him. If we followed the money, it could lead us to the source, hopefully, the same way it led me to Ms. Valmont. The many millions in her offshore account, plus her sudden disappearance after Aimee left Paris, told me she was involved. Until this trip, I did not know the sinister part she played.

The leather seat creaked as I shifted, tension coiling in my muscles. Outside, the runway lights blurred into streaks of yellow and white against the inky darkness.

“The bill for this security will be in your inbox later in the morning,” she said firmly. “Don’t call me again until you tell me you have this...I’m seldom lost for words...yes...this malignant, sadistic sociopath behind bars.”

The plane lurched forward, the engines' low rumble vibrating through the cabin. "That's the plan, Dr. Taitt. That's the plan."

She disconnected the call. I sent a message telling Jaden and Bishop we would be meeting in nine hours.

I closed my eyes, but sleep eluded me. Instead, images flashed through my mind. Aimee and I walking along the boardwalk on Anson Island, her laughter carried by the sea breeze. Us dancing at the wedding, her body warm against mine. The memory of our kiss at Hartwell Manor. Then, the gut-wrenching image of her on the floor, tucked into herself and screaming. My hand clenched into a fist, nails digging into my palm.

I wished this plane had warp speed. The sooner we pulled all these pieces together, the sooner Aimee could be free. A nagging thought spiraled in my head that she might not want me. I opened my eyes, gazing out at the night sky. The wing's flashing light pulsed rhythmically, matching the throb of anxiety in my chest. I steeled myself for the possibility. I needed to be okay with her not being in my life. I wasn't, but I would respect her wishes. Whatever they were, I would respect them.

My stomach rumbled, a sharp reminder of skipped meals. The attendant offered me a drink earlier, but I needed something more substantial now. With four hours ahead of me, I called the attendant. She provided the list of options. These ranged from grilled salmon to beef tenderloin served with sweet potato mash. There were at least three varieties of sandwiches. I selected the last option: a chicken croissant with salad. I asked for tea, knowing they should have my preferred brand on board. First Flush carried a hint of fruit. Bishop often teased me about being a tea snob. As I ate, scenarios played out in my mind, each more complex than the last.

The tea grew cold in its delicate porcelain cup as I strategized weighing risks and potential outcomes. One thing remained clear: the next twenty-four to forty-eight hours were critical. He would make his move, and we had to be ready.

The night stretched on, the plane's steady hum a constant backdrop to my restless planning. Each mile brought me closer to Etim, to answers, and to Aimee. Whether she would be part of my future remained uncertain, but her safety—and justice—were nonnegotiable. As dawn broke, painting the sky in hues of pink and gold, my resolve hardened. Whatever came next, I was prepared to face it head-on.

Forty-Five

Drago

Walking into the conference room, I was greeted by the welcoming scent of fresh coffee. Jaden's fingers flew over the keyboard as he updated the whiteboard. Bishop's face filled the screen, his brow furrowed in concentration as he spoke on another call. My hand rasped against stubble, the rough texture reminding me of my need to shave and shower.

Bishop's eyes narrowed as they swept over me. "Somebody went on a field trip." His accusing finger jabbed toward my black cargo pants and T-shirt, both creased from my being in them for almost twenty-four hours.

"Something like that." I leaned closer to the screen. "Monitor the news. An arrest should pop up soon. Low-key, but enough to set things in motion."

Jaden's fingers paused on the keyboard, his head cocking to one side. The room fell silent as I filled them in on Lazelle Valmont, her name leaving a bitter taste in my mouth.

Bishop's face contorted, disgust etching deep lines around his mouth. "How can one woman do that to another?" His voice cut through the air, sharp as a blade.

"What did you find?" I tapped the screen, redirecting us.

Jaden's report flowed, detailing their visit to Sri Lasara. He and Tanisha played their parts well, posing as journalists from the *Etim Chronicle*, interested in doing a story on Aimee Patel's roots.

Jaden continued. "Those people couldn't wait to talk. Even in that posh neighborhood, they were falling over themselves to share."

"People like their fifteen minutes of fame," Bishop said with a shrug, a hint of disdain coloring his tone.

The soft rustle of fabric filled the air as Jaden shrugged off his jacket. My eyes locked onto the names he'd scrawled on the board:

Ah-Kong

Ramdas

Thani

"Talk to us," I prompted, the words coming out more as a command than a request.

These were the three families that met our criteria. Ah-Kong was the retired president of the company where Aimee's dad worked. He was a multi-millionaire, with two sons, who both lived in Sri Lasara. One was married and the other appeared to be a confirmed bachelor and player.

He continued by informing us that Ramdas was Aimee's godfather. He was a retired minister of finance with a net worth of over three billion dollars. According to Jaden, most of his money came from agribusiness and real estate. He had one son, who was a widower. The politically ambitious son seemed interested in running for prime minister and was doing all the right things to position himself. He served in the army and was on track to be promoted to general, but rumors suggested that he would be leaving the army. His father had set up a hundred-million-dollar trust fund for him when he turned thirty.

Thani was her father's best friend and executor of his will, with a daughter Aimee's age and a son eight years older than Aimee and recently divorced. The Thani wealth was not in the same range as the others, but Thani was not hurting financially. His net worth was around seventy-five million.

Walking to the whiteboard, I asked, "Pulling all this together, what do we know?"

"This perp is older than Aimee for sure," Bishop interjected, his voice tinged with certainty.

Picking up the stylus, I sketched out a mind map with Aimee's name at the center and the events spiraling outward. The hair on my neck stood at attention, alerting me to follow my instincts, but concern caused goosebumps to dot my skin.

"Bishop, Jaden"—my voice cut through the tension— "track down each of these men's sons. I need locations, movements, everything from the last two months. I'll shower and be back in fifteen."

I burst from the room, urgency propelling me toward the penthouse. The elevator's soft whir seemed deafening in the charged silence. We were close, so close to nailing him. I could feel us closing in on him.

The TV flickered to life under my touch. Within minutes, the news banner crawled across the bottom: "Retired fashion designer Lazelle Valmont in police custody." My lips curled into a predatory smile, satisfaction coursing through my veins. "We're coming for you next," I growled.

In the shower, hot water sluiced over my body, washing away grime and fatigue. I donned all-black combat gear when I was back in my room. The familiar weight of my gun settled into my palm. I slipped my Swiss Army knife into a side pocket and kept my cell in my hand.

I snagged a pair of handcuffs, the metal cool against my fingertips as I hooked them into place. A meow made me jump and I turned to see Sebastian, his warm presence a balm to my taut nerves. My fingers sunk into his thick coat. "We'll get him, boy. Hopefully, you'll see her soon."

Hopefully.

When I returned to the conference room, Bishop and Jaden were hunched over their laptops. The air was charged by our adrenaline and determination.

"Ah-Kong's son," Jaden broke the silence, "our player guy, is living it up in Switzerland. Been gallivanting around Europe for two months."

"Report on Thani and Ramdas incoming," Bishop muttered, eyes never leaving his screen.

Okay," I said, continuing to scan the board. My gut churned with certainty. The answer was here.

. "Oh crap!" Bishop's voice thundered through my thoughts. His eyes flickered up to meet mine. "Crap, crap, crap."

A foreboding sense of doom spread through my body.

Forty-Six

Aimee

Sweat trickled down my face, each droplet a testament to my effort. Two more push-ups. Drago's voice echoed in my mind, urging me on. I collapsed onto the mat after completing my third set of twenty, muscles quivering. The thought struck me like a thunderbolt—I missed sparring with him. My arms, once soft and unimpressive, now bore the definition of consistent training. Not bulky like a weightlifter, but lean and toned.

Drago's absence gnawed at me, a persistent ache beneath my ribs. The gym, usually empty at this ungodly hour, had one other occupant, a woman running on the treadmill, her steady rhythm a counterpoint to my ragged breathing. I savored these quiet mornings. My routine—workout, shower, garden—was like an anchor in the chaos of my thoughts, especially the garden, where I could lose myself.

As I stretched, my mind wandered. Maybe I should reach out to Drago. Dinner? No, too intimate. Lunch, then. Or perhaps a visit, with the added bonus of seeing Sebastian. I stood without bracing myself; a small victory. A laugh bubbled up, unbidden, at the realization of my newfound core strength, just like Drago had said. The woman on the treadmill glanced over, curiosity in her eyes.

The gym itself was a testament to its high-end clientele. Sleek cardio machines gleamed under soft lighting, while mirrors lined the back wall, reflecting rows of yoga mats and balance balls. A weight rack stood in the corner, its heaviest weight being twenty-five pounds. At 11:00 a.m. daily, the space transformed for a guided exercise session— something I'd avoided like the plague. Working out with Drago had awakened a love for fitness I never knew I possessed, but the thought of following an instructor's peppy commands still made me cringe. And that was okay.

Longing and uncertainty warred within me as I stretched my other leg. This retreat, as healing as it had been, couldn't be my forever. Drago's face swam before my eyes, bringing with it a tidal wave of questions. What would our future look like? The only way to find out was to take that first, terrifying step. I resolved to stop by the reception desk after my shower and schedule an appointment with Dr. Taitt.

The scent of coffee lured me as I left the gym. I paused to grab a latte, watching the staff prepare for the day ahead. Salt and pepper shakers clinked as they were set in place, a mundane symphony of normalcy. Perhaps today I'd indulge in a leisurely breakfast, maybe even strike up a conversation. Many of the women here were professionals, either burned out from work or life in general. Or like me, dealing with some trauma.

Latte in hand, I jogged up to my room. The bed was already made, a habit my parents drilled into me. "Young lady, you're never to leave home with your bed unmade." I could hear the stern but loving sound of my father's words echoing in my head.

I stepped onto the patio, and the air was still slightly chilly, but the warmth of my drink added some heat as my body cooled down from my exercise. The sun crept higher, chasing away the last vestiges of night, taking some of the nip out of the air.

My damp sports bra clung to me. A shower was needed before I knocked myself out from my own sweat.

After my shower, I slipped into navy blue trousers and a matching off-the-shoulder top. Not my usual gardening attire, but perfect for a day of introspection. Instead of busying myself with plants and soil, I perched on the edge of the bed, determined to untangle the knot of my thoughts before meeting Dr. Taitt.

An hour ticked by, yet clarity remained elusive. Drago consumed my mind like a stubborn vine. One moment, I yearned for his presence; the next, doubt coiled in my stomach like a restless snake. Our potential future stretched before me, a path shrouded in fog.

The restaurant buzzed with life as I entered. Women sat alone or in small groups, some buried in books, others radiating a clear "do not disturb" energy. My eyes landed on the woman from the gym. She steeped a tea bag in her cup.

"Mind if I join you?" I asked, mustering a smile.

Her dark eyes crinkled with warmth. "Yes. Gym, right?"

"Yup. I'm the one that interrupted your workout," I said, settling into the chair. "Aimee."

"Carla."

When the server approached, my usual egg white omelet order balanced on the tip of my tongue. Instead, I heard myself say, "Can I have French toast with a side of bacon? A cappuccino also. Thanks." The small rebellion in my eating was freeing.

Carla nodded toward my phone. "You're not here to disconnect from work?"

"Working through some issues," I replied, the words inadequate yet true.

We fell into conversation. She started an online business as an influencer, and the pressure to keep up became too much. Her words painted a vivid picture of a life controlled by others' expectations. "I can do without another cellphone or device," she confessed. "I let that control my life. Or rather, people controlled my life. How to dress. Crazy diets. Don't talk about the competition."

As we spoke, we barely noticed that the restaurant had emptied around us, and we lingered in our little bubble.

The vibration of my phone shattered our moment. The screen lit up with a familiar name. "Excuse me. I need to take this call."

She nodded as I answered. "Hi. Sorry, I did not—" I began, but the voice on the other end cut me off.

"I'm in trouble. But I didn't do it. I swear, Aimee. I didn't. He said..."

My heart raced, blood rushing in my ears. "Sorry, Carla. I have to go," I managed, already half-standing.

"Who said what?" I asked.

As I listened, I remembered a little object I had stolen—let's say borrowed—that was in my suitcase.

Forty-Seven

Drago

Bishop read the report. Kiran Ramdas entered Etim on a diplomatic passport with full diplomatic immunity eight weeks ago. Bishop continued reading while Jaden switched his attention to tracking his movements.

"Get a location on him. I want to know everything he did in the last forty-eight hours."

Picking up the phone, I called Shae Anson. After two rings, he answered, "Drago."

"I need you to pull some strings. I want to know what Kiran Ramdas is doing in Etim. He's here with full diplomatic immunity. That means he's a guest of the state."

"Let me find Jordan. Does this have anything to do with Aimee?"

Letting out a breath, "My gut tells me he's at the center of this entire thing."

After disconnecting the call, Bishop pulled up his stats on the screen.

Name: Kiran Amit Ramdas

Age: 49

Wife: Married 4 1/2 years

Widower:5 months

Job: Lieutenant General and Non-Executive Director of Ramdas Holding

Volunteer: Donated $250,000 to children's charities in honor of his wife

"The man's a saint. He even plays Santa at Christmas," Bishop muttered.

Watching the screen as the information populated it, I remarked, "Don't forget Ted Bundy volunteered at a crisis hotline."

Jaden, his eyes also riveted to the screen, responded, "True, Boss."

Residence: London, Antigua, Ireland, and Paris

Net worth: Undisclosed, speculated to be close to $1 billion

Special Assignment: Etim Military Surveillance Team

Bishop continued typing and more information filled the screen. Jaden jumped up. "Call Leila." There was urgency in his voice.

Standing straighter, ignoring the claws grabbing at my chest, I asked, "Why?" My eyes narrowed in on Jaden. Bishop's hand stilled.

Grabbing his jacket, Jaden said, "She's in the military. Surveillance, to be precise. When we went to Vibrant Bowls, she mentioned having a temporary commanding officer who was here on a special assignment."

"What area of surveillance does she work in?" Bishop asked as I picked up my cell.

Jaden shrugged on his jacket. "Drones. She's trained to operate drones."

My heart sank. The phone vibrated with an incoming call. After answering it, I felt as if the world had collapsed around me. "Gone? How do you mean gone?" I shouted.

A heavy silence filled the room. Everything stood still, even Bishop on screen.

Gone.

They must be joking. That would be one sick joke to play.

Aimee.

Gone.

Forty-Eight

Aimee

It was strange being in my home. Two months had passed since I'd last slept here, and this marked only my second visit during that time. My suitcase was packed and rested by the door. On the breakfast nook where Topaz and I shared countless girl sessions, stood a bottle of red wine and a glass, its rim stained with lipstick.

Turning, I returned upstairs. Resting my hand on a perfectly made bed with the luxurious blue comforter and pillows piled against the headboard in the same formation as I left them many weeks ago, I reached under the bedside table until my hand grasped what I wanted. Pulling it out, I tucked it into the waist of my pants at the small of my back and covered it with my sweater.

The sun filtered through the window, although it was after 6:00 p.m. In a few months, it would be dark. I left the bedroom, leaving the door ajar. Standing at the top of the stairs, my skin tingled as I took one careful step after another down. A blend of woody sweetness permeated the air, a scent that was absent moments ago.

As my feet reached the middle step, a man, whom I had only seen in a picture less than two hours ago, glanced at me, then my suitcase. Drinking my wine, he asked, "Are you going somewhere?"

"Who are you?"

"You're even more beautiful than I remembered."

Trying not to throw up, I repeated my question. I would not let him win.

"Who are you?"

Sitting at the breakfast bar, he extended his hand, but I refused to step forward to take it.

"Seems you're making yourself at home," I remarked and not in a hospitable way.

As he poured himself another glass of wine, I remained out of reach, and I watched the man who had made my life a living hell. Gray streaks ran through his black hair. He was testimony that beauty was only skin deep because he was an attractive man. His looks had probably fooled many people.

Setting down the glass, he said, "You have fine taste in wine. Black currants." He passed the glass under his nose again. "A hint of vanilla."

Keeping my distance and taking my phone out of my back pocket, I demanded, "Tell me who the hell you are and why me, before I call the police."

"You don't want to do that." His lips curved slowly upward, malice blazing in his eyes, turning the smile into something cold and threatening. "It's all your father's fault. That old man was stubborn."

"Dad?" The word slipped out, barely a whisper. My mind raced, trying to catch up with what he was implying.

Standing, he was more like 6'2″.

The air seemed to thicken as he stepped closer. "Stay where you are, or I will call the police." My voice shook, but I gripped the phone in my hand tighter.

"Sweet girl," he cooed, waving a small, black sleek device, a remote of some kind. "If you do that, all the hard work your friend Topaz did will have been in vain."

"What?"

Holding the device in one hand, with the other, he formed a fist and flicked it open, accompanying it with the word "Poof."

Forty-Nine

Aimee

"You didn't answer me. Who are you and what are you doing in my house?"

Holding onto the device, he extended his right hand again, which I totally ignored. His eyes gleamed, dark and sharp. But beneath the surface, something shifted—his gaze darted for a moment, then narrowed again, like the control he held was fragile, ready to slip.

Hand still outstretched, he said. "Let me formally introduce myself. We've met before, but you don't remember," he said with a smirk on his face. How I would like to wipe it off with the bottom of my shoe!

"I'm Kiran. Kiran Amit Ramdas. Sorry for the long delay in introductions. Over five years. My bad."

"I could have done without the first one. Actually, all of them."

Shaking his head, he dropped his hand when he saw I wasn't going to take it. His eyes fixed on mine, wide and erratic, as his words tumbled out. "Your dad...my dad... They sealed this long before you were even a thought. Firstborns, bound by a promise. But you? You ruined everything. You came along too late. I was already twenty, full of life, while you were a screaming infant. My dad settled for being your godfather, and what did I get? Nothing."

Pushing his free hand into his pants pocket, he continued. "But I didn't care. Not at the time. I thought I had everything. Women, so many numbers I could've written a phone book. A *phone book!*" His laugh burst out, sharp and jagged, as if he found it all too funny. "Then there you were again. The moment you won Miss Etim, I knew it. I *knew* you were mine. It was destiny! Do you understand? *Destiny!*" His voice, which had risen in pitch, cracked, as he leaned forward, eyes wide with a manic gleam.

"But your dad—*that* old fool—he tried to stop it. Said I was too old for you when I contacted him about the promise made between our fathers." He let out another hollow laugh, louder, more erratic. "Age gap? *Ha!* He never heard of age-gap romance! He didn't understand what we are—what we're *meant* to be. But I do. I *always* have." His shoulders shook as a crazed laugh spilled out of him in bursts, uncontrollable, as if the very idea of it all drove him over the edge. "It was always you and me. Always." His mouth curved into a disturbing smile.

His eyes roamed my body, lingering on my face and then my breasts. The little black gadget remained in his hand.

"It was a sad thing to end his life. He went peacefully. The car didn't blow up. Only ran off the road."

"You killed my father?"

"I removed an obstacle." Smiling, he added, "I removed many obstacles. Including my now-late wife."

Taking another sip of the wine and resting the glass down on the breakfast nook, he continued. "My dad needed me to settle down. I married a woman; she had your eyes. I pretended it was you every time we made love. But it was not the same. She, too, met an untimely death. For the last two years, the doctors tried to figure out what was wrong."

Laughing and waving the remote, he said, "I was slowly poisoning her. If I'm going to be the next leader of my country, I need my queen—not some imposter." He threw his head back, his laughter splintering into high-pitched gasps that made my skin crawl.

"You're sick."

"No, Aimee." He paused, blinking rapidly, his head jerking as if trying to shake off a fog. "I'm... obsessed. Obsessed with you," he muttered, his words dragging. He pressed his hand against his temple.

He inched closer to me, and I allowed him. "Why did you..." I couldn't get the words out. "Why did you..."

"Have sex with you?" Throwing back his head, he laughed then said, "Not sex. I worshipped your body. You were a little out of it, but next time you will remember. I enjoyed being your first." His words slurred. "Also, I will be your only."

His black eyes settled on me. "You lost our baby. How could you?" He stretched his hand to touch my face, and I slapped it away.

"What's that?" I asked, tilting my head in the direction of the gadget in his hand.

"Something that goes BOOM! And it will do so over the Anson Resort. Unless you come with me," he said, now tracing my cheek with his fingers.

"Are you too selfish, Aimee, to do something for Topaz?" His fingers shook as he trailed his hand down my neck, toward my breast. "One kiss, Aimee. One kiss."

When he leaned in to kiss me, I kneed him in his groin and slapped the hand clutching the remote.

"You bit—" he started to say.

The remote flew out of his hand, landing somewhere near the living room. I sprinted after it, adrenaline surging through my veins. His footsteps thundered behind me, heavy and uneven, but he was still coming. I spotted the remote and lunged for it, my fingers brushing against its edge when he crashed into me from behind, knocking the wind out of me.

We hit the floor hard. His weight pinned me down, and I could feel his breath on my neck, hot and ragged. He grabbed my shoulder, roughly flipping me over. His eyes, wide and dilated, locked onto mine. "You drugged me," he growled, his voice thick, but his grip on my throat tightened. Even drugged, his strength was terrifying.

Panic gripped me, but Drago's training echoed in my mind. Hit and escape, target the weakest point. I twisted my body, bringing my right hand up sharply, and jabbed my thumb into his eye with all the force I could muster.

He roared in pain, his hold on my throat loosening just enough for me to squirm out from under him. I scrambled to my feet, but his hand shot out, grabbing my ankle in a vice-like grip. His lips curled into a sickening smile. Still gripping my ankle, he lunged toward the remote that had skittered under the chair.

Desperation gripped me. My hand instinctively slid to my back, where the cold metal of my gun waited. In one swift motion, I pulled it out, aimed, and squeezed the trigger. The gun kicked back, the sound of the shot deafening in the enclosed space.

He froze, eyes wide. Blood seeped through his shirt, but the grip on my ankle remained. He pressed the button, and a vibration shook the building. The sick psycho tossed the little black remote from his hands, swaying either from the loss of blood or the drug that I poured into the wine, and lunged for me. I aimed my gun at him again.

Fifty

Drago

Shae arranged for his project manager to leave a vehicle. The driver's door was slightly ajar, and the key hidden under the mat. I threw the key onto the passenger seat. The engine roared to life with a quick press of the start button. The tires skid slightly on the gravel. Jaden and Leila were otherwise occupied. Aimee was my priority.

Dr. Taitt's call still echoed in my mind—her voice strained, words clipped. "She's gone." Those two words sent a shiver down my spine. The gears in my mind started turning, piecing together the hastened movements of a man desperate to wrap up loose ends, especially after Lazelle Valmont's arrest. With Minerva, I couldn't save her; it was out of my control. But Aimee—if anything happened to her—it would be my fault.

God, don't let her die. The steering wheel groaned under the force of my grip. The road blurred as the car raced toward

Aimee's house, every second ticking by like a countdown. The lights inside were a beacon, but they also signaled danger. I shoved the gear stick into park the moment the house loomed ahead, leaping out and covering the distance with long strides, urgency propelling me forward.

My hand instinctively reached for the gun at my side, fingers brushing against the metal. The weight of it anchored me. I kept the weapon hidden, as I did not want to draw the attention of the villas' guests. If they stepped outside, they'd see nothing more than a man on a mission, not the storm brewing inside me. I could feel my muscles coiled tight, ready to strike.

The front door was just ahead, but then—*crack!* A shot pierced the air, sharp and final. A breath later, the ground trembled with the force of an explosion, a concussive wave that hit like a punch to the chest. The blast jerked my body back, but I stayed on my feet, mind racing.

Aimee!

The world narrowed to that single thought: the echo of the shot and the blast reverberating in my ears, pushing me forward despite the fear gnawing at the edges of my resolve.

"No!" The word tore from my throat, primal and raw. The door splintered under my boot, the force of the kick sending it crashing inward. Gun raised, finger steady on the trigger, I scanned the room. Kiran Amit Ramdas—there in the flesh. His eyes locked onto Aimee. Blood seeped through his shirt, but still, he lunged, desperation driving him forward. Aimee's gun wavered in her grasp. The sight of her—so vulnerable, so close to being taken from me—ignited something savage inside me.

Kiran's lips twisted into a sneer, his eyes still fixed on Aimee. "You don't have what it takes to kill me," he slurred, arrogance dripping from every syllable in spite of his unsteady gait.

Aiming my gun at him, I said, "That's why she has me."

The shot rang out, another deafening crack that echoed through the room, followed by the dull thud of his body collapsing onto Aimee.

Her scream shattered my heart. "Get him off me! Get him off me!" she screamed, each word a plea that cut deep.

I was beside her in an instant, hands moving swiftly, roughly, to get Kiran's lifeless body off hers. His body, the dead weight of a man who'd moments ago threatened everything, rolled to the floor. Aimee's arms were around my neck, her sobs racking her frame and mingling with the rapid beats of my heart. Every instinct screamed to protect, to shield her from this nightmare that had come to life.

Jaden burst into the room with Leila close behind. They froze at the sight of us—Aimee clinging to me, her tears soaking through my shirt. Jaden's eyes met mine, a silent exchange.

"Boss, it's been neutralized," he said, his voice steady, grounding.

My gaze flickered between Jaden and Leila. The adrenaline was still coursing through my body. "That blast...was in my head?"

Leila stepped forward, calm and precise. "Sir, I redirected the drone. Overrode the commands and took control before it detonated."

The room spun with the aftermath—blood spattered across the floor; a side table overturned. But Aimee...Aimee was alive, warm in my arms. A silent prayer rose within me, a breath of relief. "Thank you, Jesus."

The front door creaked open and all three of us snapped to attention, guns raised.

Fifty-One

Drago

Entering the room with two men dressed in black, Crown Prince Jordan's eyes swept over the chaos, lingering on each detail with a sharp, calculating gaze. "Drago, it seems we've got one hell of an international relations issue on our hands." The tension in the room shifted as everyone lowered their guns, but Jordan remained unflinching, as though the weapons never phased him.

"Kiran Amit Ramdas was being groomed to be the next Prime Minister of Sri Lasara," Jordan stated, his voice carrying a weight that pressed down on the room.

"Guess they'll have to find someone else," I replied, my tone edged with the cold finality of the situation.

Jordan approached, his steps purposeful. He crouched down to Aimee, his demeanor softening slightly as he took in her shaken state. Focusing on me, he said, "Remind me to never invite myself to your house unannounced. Your greeting leaves much to be desired." A wry smile tugged at the corner of his mouth. But as his eyes shifted to Aimee, the levity disappeared. "I'll handle this. Drago and his team will get you out of here."

Aimee's grip around my neck tightened, her knuckles pressing into my skin. Her eyes, wide as if searching for something to anchor her as if his words had slipped past the barrier she'd retreated behind.

Jordan stood, his expression hardening as he shifted back into command. "I need you all to leave," he ordered, pulling out his phone and dialing quickly. "You were never here."

I hoisted Aimee to her feet, her body trembling as if her strength had drained away. Leila rushed forward, wrapping Aimee in a tight embrace. I watched, holding myself back, every instinct screaming to pull Aimee back into my arms, to keep her hidden away where no one could reach her again.

"Boss, I'll bring the vehicle," Jaden said, already moving toward the door.

Jordan's brow furrowed as he continued barking orders into the phone, his voice low but urgent, the authority in his tone unmistakable.

Aimee shifted, leaving Leila's embrace, and returned to me, her arms circling my waist. I steadied her, offering her support and comfort. As we reached the door, Jordan's voice halted me when he shouted, "Drago!" I turned and met his gaze—a cold, steely look that cut through the distance like a blade. His eyes narrowed and locked onto mine with an intensity that left no room for doubt. No softness. "You better take good care of her. I wouldn't want to revoke your license to conduct business here."

Jordan's eyes held mine for a moment longer before he turned back to the task at hand.

Fifty-Two

Aimee

The roar of the engines filled my ears as the plane climbed higher, becoming a silver speck against the sky. My heart clenched. As much as I wanted him to stay, I knew I needed this time to myself—to heal.

I turned away from the runway and walked toward the beach, grateful for the concierge's offer to take my luggage to the villa. The waters off Etim were beautiful, but the waters in the Caribbean were nothing short of magical.

Waves lapped at the shore, their soothing rhythm matching my steps. Up ahead, I spotted the familiar silhouette of the cabanas—wood polished and gleaming despite exposure to the rain and sun. The white fabric billowed in the wind, straining against the ropes that held it in place. The sun beat down on my shoulders as I approached the nearest cabana, eager to escape its heat. I eased into the hammock, gently swinging back and forth.

When I told Topaz that I wanted to spend some time here, I hadn't expected it would be the very same night.

I closed my eyes, letting the rhythm of the waves crashing on the shore wash over me. The salty breeze tickled my face, and slowly, a smile tugged at my lips. The tension that gripped me for so long began to loosen. Finally, the weight lifted—*I was free.* The path that led here had been twisted and uncertain, nothing I imagined, but maybe that was the point. Maybe this was God's way of reminding me—reminding us—that He held the reins all along.

The ocean's steady pulse called to me, its cool depths promising an escape, a moment of pure release. The thought of diving in, feeling the water engulf me, was almost irresistible. How much could change in twenty-four hours? The memory of Leila's frantic call flashed through my mind. Kiran had cornered her, demanding that she lure me to the villa alone, or else he would spread lies—convincing lies—that she sold Etim's cutting-edge drone technology to a cartel. Even I might have doubted her innocence if I hadn't come to know her over these months. Anyone would have questioned her when they saw the mysterious three million in her account, transferred from an account in the Cayman Islands.

I laughed softly to myself. Leila no longer needed to be my employee. She got the last laugh on him. I doubted Jordan would make her give back the money. None would be the wiser. She could finally pursue her dream of designing jewelry.

The setting sun dipped lower, casting long shadows on the sand, a silent reminder that it had been hours since I last ate. On the way back to the villa, the glow of a small bar caught my eye, and I wandered inside, ordering a tuna sandwich with a garden salad and sparkling water. The server handed me the bottle, unopened as I had requested—I hadn't shaken the habit, and maybe never would. Somehow, that thought didn't scare me as much as it had before.

I bit into the sandwich, and the taste of fresh tuna and crisp lettuce filled my mouth. It was so good, making me wonder why I had starved myself all day. The sandwich vanished in two bites. Either it was small, or I was ravenous. I sipped the water slowly, each cool swallow grounding me in the present, though my mind drifted to the decisions that had brought me here.

Leila picked me up from the retreat, and we went to a small café where she filled me in on everything—about the missing drones, the email he had already typed, threatening that she would spend the rest of her life locked away in Etim's prison. His plan was for her to trick me into coming to the villa, but instead, she told me the truth. I should have called Drago, but I figured Dr. Taitt would call once she realized I was missing.

This was something I needed to do. I needed to face Kiran Amit Ramdas. My tormentor. I was tired. One way or another, I was prepared to end it, even if it meant my death. I could no longer live in hiding. That was my one shot, and I grasped it, praying for the best.

Every detail had been planned.

I could still see the vial in my hand. I emptied the vial I had taken from Tanisha without permission when I visited her lab. Technically, I stole it. Back then, I thought it might come in handy. It certainly did.

The wine glass, the lipstick mark. I placed the lipstick print on the glass and poured some wine into the glass, to make it look like I had drunk some already.

His body had fought against the effects of the drug. If I hadn't been so precise, so prepared, I wouldn't be here now, sipping water in a half-empty bar. An icy shiver traced down my spine, despite the rays of the setting sun on my back. His ability to withstand the drug—that must have been years of military training kicking in.

All of this happened because his sick, twisted mind thought we were fated to be together.

How do I even process all of this?

Fifty-Three

Drago

Leaving Aimee on that island and returning to Etim was one of the hardest things I had ever done. If I could have stayed hidden without her knowing I was there, I would have. But I knew she needed this time. I took comfort in knowing that the resort's security was top-notch, headed by a retired Navy SEAL.

We overnighted in Barbados to give the crew the required rest time. I could have done it in Miami as well, but I liked the idea of being close to her. Arriving this morning, I showered and came straight to the office. I monitored the news yesterday—nothing. All of this unfolded on Wednesday evening, but I didn't doubt Jordan's ability to handle the situation.

"Boss," Jaden said, pulling up today's agenda on the screen. "It's Friday. You look like you're going to crack any moment.

Tanisha and I are going to watch a play at the amphitheater. Want to join us?"

"You watch plays?"

"You do when your wife says she wants to—if you know what's good for you."

I shook my head. "I must really look like crap."

As we settled into the conference room, Bishop's face finally popped up on the screen. It was odd, as he normally waited for us. Bishop had a thing for being super punctual. The background caught my eye immediately—an unmade bed, rumpled sheets telling their own story. A woman's voice floated through, followed by a door clicking shut.

I exchanged a glance with Jaden before addressing the elephant in the room. "Bishop, you're looking...relaxed."

Bishop's jaw tightened. "Just embracing my new philosophy: relationships are overrated."

"Rough night?" Jaden probed, his tone a mix of concern and curiosity.

"Can we get to business?" Bishop growled.

I nodded, respecting the clear boundary. "All right, gentlemen. We've got two potential assignments on the table."

Bishop oversaw and specialized in cybersecurity and terrorism; we took on a maximum of two active field assignments at any time. The sum being paid was not the main motivator—at times it was the heinous nature of the crime. We agreed on the father who wanted his daughter extracted from a cult group known for sacrificing women once a year. He feared for his daughter's life. The second one wasn't our usual type: a politician who believed his wife was cheating—with his opponent.

Bishop leaned forward, his earlier irritation giving way to focus. "I'll take the wife case."

I frowned. "That's in Europe. Wouldn't it make more sense for Jaden to handle that one?"

"I'll take the case," Bishop repeated.

Jaden jumped in. "I'm good with the cult extraction. Colombia's lovely this time of year."

I raised a brow at their quick decisions but didn't push. "All right. It's your call."

I debated whether to pursue the matter with Bishop now but seeing the set of his jaw and his lips in a straight line, I knew this was a no-go zone at the moment. Respecting each other's boundaries was important in our relationship and business.

"Anything else we need to cover?" Bishop leaned forward, one hand hovering near the mouse, his gaze darting to the corner of the screen with the "End Call" button as if he couldn't wait to click it.

"Actually," I turned to Jaden, "what's the status on hiring a receptionist?"

Jaden squirmed in his seat. "Still looking for the right fit."

"How many interviews so far?" I pressed.

"About sixty," he admitted sheepishly.

Bishop let out a low whistle. "Damn, Jaden. What are you looking for? A unicorn?"

"What happened to that woman from last week?" I asked, exasperated.

Jaden's expression turned defensive. "She had two unpaid parking tickets."

I pinched the bridge of my nose. "Jaden, I swear... I want you in your office and not outside intimidating our clients."

My phone buzzed—the alert I'd set for news on Kiran Amit Ramdas. As I read the report, a grim satisfaction settled over me.

"Well, gentlemen," I said, looking up from my phone. "It seems Lieutenant General Ramdas won't be leading any political parties. He's been found dead of a 'massive heart attack'."

Bishop's eyes narrowed. "Heart attack, huh? How...sad."

At least one part was true... Jordan found him dead.

Fifty-Four

Aimee

Dr. Taitt suggested picking up a hobby. I made progress with jogging—each morning, the steady rhythm of my feet hitting the sand was a reminder that I could move forward. But crocheting? That was a different story. In the two weeks I'd been tucked away on this island, nestled in the quiet embrace of the ocean breeze, I'd been following N Creations on YouTube, trying to coax some semblance of order out of tangled yarn. Yet, despite my best efforts, I hadn't managed to produce a single thing.

My gaze drifted to the small pile of yarn and hook on the table beside me. The keyring—so small, so deceptively simple—lay there, half-formed and abandoned, like all my other attempts. How hard could it be to crochet a keyring? I'd thought it would be easy, a mindless task to keep my hands busy. But the chain stitches always came out uneven, the loops never lined up right, and the yarn constantly slipped off my hook. Apparently, it was harder than I imagined, and it mocked me from its unfinished state. The lady on N Creations made it look so easy.

But I'm stubborn, and today, I'm determined. Today, we're making hearts.

As I picked up the crochet hook, the door chimed, cutting through the quiet. I glanced around the villa, my eyes landing on the bouquet from earlier—twelve calla lilies and twelve red roses, their petals a perfect contrast of white and deep red, still fresh in the morning light. Drago's doing, of course. He couldn't be sending more flowers, could he?

Pausing the video, I set aside the crochet hook and walked to the door. As I peered through the peephole, I expected to see another flower arrangement, but instead, there was a gift bag. Opening the door to the concierge, who handed me the bag with a polite smile, I thanked him and then closed the door gently behind me.

Back on the sofa, I placed the bag beside the unfinished crochet projects and glanced at the clock. Thirty minutes until my first official session with Dr. Hayes. My stomach twisted at the thought. Even though Dr. Taitt assured me of her professionalism, the idea of opening up about my deepest fears—about sex, intimacy, and whether I'd ever want to be touched in that way—made my chest tighten.

Twenty-eight minutes before my session. I reached into the bag, fingers brushing against soft, crinkling tissue paper in a delicate shade of light blue. Beneath the layers, my fingers touched something thin and solid—a book. When I pulled it out, the title caught my eye: *Thirty-One Bible Verses to Transform Your Mind.*

I opened the cover, the faint scent of new paper rising as I did. There, in neat, familiar handwriting, was an inscription: *As you read these verses, may they help in the healing process. Love, Topaz.* The thoughtful message echoed in my head.

A small smile tugged at my lips as I turned to the first page.

2 Timothy 1:7

For God gave us a spirit not of fear but of power and love and self-control.

There were lines underneath to write my thoughts. I reflected on the verse and fear gripped me. The fear of being inadequate sexually. Not wanting to be touched. How would I function in a relationship?

Ruminating caused the time to go faster, and my phone alarm went off, notifying me of the session. Going over to the dining room table, I logged onto the call. Her warm brown eyes greeted me, her glasses pushed up onto her head like a headband.

"Aimee, it's nice to see you again. Especially since our first session was cut short."

You can do this.

Removing her glasses from her head, she placed them on the bridge of her nose as she reviewed a file. She informed me that Dr. Taitt updated her on all that transpired since our attempted session.

"Do you feel ready for this session?"

Ready? Ready meant prepared, equipped to handle whatever came next. But nothing about this seemed manageable. The very idea of discussing intimacy tightened my chest—I wanted to bury these thoughts and emotions, not excavate them.

Leaning forward on the table, I replied, "To be honest, I'm far from ready. I may never be ready. But for me to have the life I want, this is something I must deal with." The words emerged steadily, a small victory in a battle far from over.

She nodded, her expression a careful blend of understanding and firmness as she started and guided the conversation. The next forty-five minutes peeled back layers I had meticulously built around me. Defenses crumbled, exposing vulnerabilities that were more terrifying than liberating.

She closed the folder. Her eyes, patient and searching, met mine. "What is your biggest fear right now?"

The dreaded question loomed. I could no longer avoid it. Wetting my lips, I spoke. "That I won't want to be touched in an intimate way—that I'll be repulsed by sex."

What man would want a woman who couldn't please him in the bedroom?

Fifty-Five

Drago

Stepping off the lift after the outer door slid open, I was greeted by the cool air of the penthouse. Sebastian, as usual, was waiting. He barely gave me a glance before turning on his paws and swishing his tail in clear disapproval. I was not Aimee. His disappointment was palpable. His eyes lingered on the door, as if expecting her to walk through any second, and I could almost hear him blaming me for her absence.

"Come, boy. I miss her too." The words fell into the empty room, the silence swallowing them up. It had been a month—thirty days of no contact, no call, just the haunting memories of our last moments together. We met under the most trying circumstances, adrenaline and danger swirling around us like a storm. But was there more to it? Was it real for her, or just the desperation of the moment, the raw instinct to survive? For me, it was so much more. Every week, I sent flowers, hoping that each petal would carry a piece of me to her, that she would remember, that I wouldn't fade with each passing day. The urge to fly to her, to see her face, even for a minute, gnawed at me constantly.

I dropped onto the sofa, the cushions barely yielding under the weight of my thoughts. Bishop wrapped up his case with the adulterous wife, a job well done. Jaden messaged me yesterday, saying he was on his way home. The thought of Jaden refusing to hire a receptionist crossed my mind, a point of frustration that simmered under the surface. If I had to endure another meeting with Bishop in some random hotel room, I'd find a way to drag his stubborn butt over here. We needed to hire at least two more field operatives, and that wasn't a job I could keep putting off.

The decision between takeout or reheating leftovers loomed, both options equally unappealing. The hunger was there, but the energy to do anything about it wasn't. I forced myself to move, but as I did, the soft chime of the elevator reached my ears, followed by the quiet click of the penthouse door opening. My heart skipped a beat, then kicked into a wild rhythm.

And there she was.

"Aimee."

Her name escaped my lips before I could stop it. She stood there, framed by the doorway in a white T-shirt that fit her like a second skin and a black, full-flowing skirt with a slit that teased the length of her leg.

"Drago."

She spoke my name, and the world narrowed to the two of us. Everything else—the city, the cases, Bishop, the nonexistent receptionist—faded into the background.

Sebastian jumped off the bar stool and dashed toward her, his tail a blur of excitement. She bent down, scooping him up, and I couldn't take my eyes off her. She was really here.

She buried her head in his fur, her shoulders relaxing in a way that made my chest tighten with a different kind of jealousy. That damn cat was getting what I wanted so badly. Her suitcase stood by the entrance; I crossed the room to retrieve it. The simple act confirmed the reality that she was here in my home.

Still holding Sebastian, she glanced up at me. "I should have called. But I wanted to surprise you."

"A welcome surprise," I said, the words carrying more weight than they should have.

She set Sebastian down, but the cat wound around her ankles like a magnet. She took a step closer to me, lifting her gaze to meet mine. "It was a long flight. Too nervous to eat, but I'm hungry now. Can I invite you to dinner?"

Stepping forward, I closed the distance between us, our bodies close enough that I could almost feel the heat radiating from her. A sheet of paper could have barely slipped between us. The words that danced on the tip of my tongue were anything but appropriate, so I settled for, "Yes. You can invite me, but I will pay."

Her eyes locked with mine, something unspoken passing between us. "I'm not ready to go home. I know Leila and Tanisha went in and restored everything. But the truth is, I don't know if I'll be able to live there. Topaz's parents' hotel, The Topaz Royale, is fully booked for the next two weeks because of conferences."

I traced the line of her chin, the simple touch a promise of more. "You can stay as long as you wish."

As she walked to the guest room, I pray that my restraint held, because I knew beyond a shadow of a doubt, I wanted this woman in so many ways.

Fifty-Six

Aimee

The server uncorked the bottle with a practiced twist and poured the wine, filling the glasses before leaving the bottle to chill in the wine bucket. My gaze lingered on Drago—the sharp lines of his jaw softened by the five o'clock stubble. The way the subtle grays now threaded through his dark hair added an edge of distinction. Those gray hairs, I mused, might have appeared a little sooner because of me. The thought brought a strange mix of guilt and affection, knowing the trials we had faced together.

I raised my glass, the cool rim brushing my lips as I took a sip. The wine's crisp, slightly fruity taste washed over my tongue, a welcome distraction from the nervous energy simmering beneath my calm exterior. Lowering the glass, I allowed my eyes to roam over him, taking in every detail, every familiar feature that had become so dear to me. "Thank you," I said, my voice steady but full of unspoken depth.

He tilted his head slightly, one brow arching in that way that always made me smile. "No thanks—"

I cut him off with a shake of my head. "Drago, I can't begin to express my gratitude. You took me into your home, taught me to defend myself." I brought the glass to my lips again, savoring the wine before continuing. "You'll be glad to know I can jog for a whole sixteen minutes now. A long way from the two minutes that nearly killed me."

His laughter broke the air. Drago didn't laugh often, but when he did, it was a balm to my spirit, a reminder of the lightness that could exist between us despite everything.

"That, Ms. Aimee Patel, I would have to see with my own two eyes."

"Tomorrow morning at 5:30 a.m. And if you beat me, you owe me breakfast from a café of my choosing."

He reached for the menu, the corners of his mouth twitching with amusement. "Doesn't the loser pay?"

"Only when the odds are even. But I know I don't have a chance. I'm hoping to make it to eighteen minutes. When I can run for twenty minutes, it'll be a significant accomplishment. I'll have achieved my goal."

He shook his head, a smile playing on his lips as the server returned to take our order. We settled on a tapas platter to share, the muted hum of conversations and the soft clinking of glassware creating a backdrop to our evening. Leaning back against the plush padding of the booth, I let out a breath I didn't realize I was holding. "Most of all, I thank you for giving me the space over the last month to work through and process my thoughts. I had two weekly sessions with Dr. Taitt and another therapist she referred me to." The name Dr. Hayes lingered at the edge of my mind, but I pushed it aside—tonight wasn't the time to delve into those sessions.

He leaned forward, his expression serious, his eyes locking onto mine. "It was hard as hell. Being away from you was hard, Aimee. It's nothing I ever want to experience again."

"I have so much baggage—"

"I can handle—"

"Let me finish. I have so much baggage. You know all that happened to me. I wondered how you would view me."

Drago reached across the table, his hands warm as they closed over mine. "Aimee, you want to know how I see you?"

I nodded, even though knowing the question was rhetorical.

"You're strong. Brave. Determined. Not willing to give up, even when people doubt you. Loving. Beautiful inside and out. Also, a stealer of cats."

A small smile tugged at my lips, but underneath, the familiar unease stirred. A dark corner of my mind whispered I was broken, tainted.

The server returned, placing our platter before us: a spread of fried calamari, stuffed mushrooms, lamb kebabs, and two small bowls of Greek salad. We ate, the conversation light and easy as Drago recounted how Sebastian had claimed my room as his own. We laughed, we joked, but beneath it all, the truth weighed heavily on my chest. If we were to have a real relationship, I needed to come clean. The courage I'd been building all evening needed to see me through tonight.

As we left the restaurant, Drago's hand found the small of my back, his touch grounding me in a way that brought both comfort and resolve. The night air was cool against my skin as I led us toward one of my favorite places in Etim, the amphitheater.

"Jaden and Tanisha invited me to a production here a few weeks ago, but I passed."

"Never miss a free production. Topaz and I love it here. We came often to talk." I tilted my face upward, the stars above twinkling like distant promises, a reminder of the vastness of the world beyond our troubles.

"Come. Let's sit."

Despite wearing a Brunello Cucinelli pants, Drago settled down beside me on the stone steps, a move that would surely horrify his stylist. Around us, people sat in clusters, some with picnic baskets, others enjoying ice cream from the vendors scattered around for the summer months.

I rested my head on Drago's shoulder, and the steady rise and fall of his breathing became a soothing rhythm against the chaos in my mind. I exhaled slowly, the words bubbling up from a place I had tried to ignore.

"You're wrong, you know. So wrong." His body tensed at my words, the muscles beneath his shirt hardening as he braced himself. "Some part of me is broken, and I don't know if I want it fixed."

Fifty-Seven

Drago

It had been a week since Shae Anson contacted us to contract our cybersecurity services for the Anson Group in Europe, including the one slated to open here in Etim. It had also been a week since Aimee confessed that she must be broken. Her words lingered in my mind like a persistent echo, especially the part about feeling no remorse over the death of Kiran Amit Ramdas. We all kept calling him by his full name, for some strange reason. But it wasn't only Kiran Amit Ramdas's death that haunted her; it was the mixed emotions surrounding the child she never knew. A life she mourned, yet in the same breath, found relief in its absence.

As I reviewed the contract changes Shae requested, my focus drifted, the words on the screen blurring as thoughts of Aimee crept in. Her voice, quiet but resolute, replayed in my head: "I'm rotten, too, because I know I couldn't have kept the baby." The words had weighed heavily on her, each one a burden she carried alone. "But I couldn't have aborted it. I would have placed it up for adoption. But what mother would give away her own child?"

Without the looming threat, we started to rediscover each other, spending time together in a way that was both new and familiar. She worked remotely, still avoiding the duplex, as if crossing that threshold would somehow undo the progress she made. She mentioned a meeting with Leila later this week at the site to receive inventory. I decided to accompany her, though she hadn't asked. The thought of her facing that alone wasn't an option.

Lost in these thoughts, I didn't realize how much I had been wishing to see her until she appeared in my office doorway, as if summoned by sheer will. She walked in, carrying a box, the aroma of warm, buttery pastries trailing behind her like a promise. The scent filled the room, rich and inviting, stirring a hunger I hadn't realized was there—both for the food and for her.

I pushed back my chair and crossed the room. The box remained in her hand, her gaze lifting to mine. Without a word, I leaned in, pressing a kiss to her cheek. The softness of her skin beneath my lips was a reminder of everything I wanted but was holding back. "You're a sight for tired eyes," I said, meaning every word. The fatigue of the week seemed to dissolve in her presence, but I knew she wasn't ready for more than this—a hand held, a kiss on the cheek. The part of me that wanted to pull her close, to claim those peach-colored lips, stayed restrained, caged by the understanding that she needed time.

"Seeing that this will be a long meeting, I popped down to the bakery and ordered an assortment of pastries," she said, her tone light, though the shadows under her eyes hinted at the weight she still carried.

"Long meeting?" I asked, raising a brow.

"Yup. Topaz wants everything to be perfect for the opening of the resort. So, buckle in for at least three hours."

A smile tugged at the corner of my mouth as I returned to my tablet, preparing for the meeting. Jaden would be joining us, and I already warned Bishop to keep his video background clean—no rumpled beds in sight, or I'd strangle him through the screen.

Aimee's voice broke through my thoughts. "You're giving off some serious vibes there," she remarked, her gaze sharp, as if she could see right through me.

"Jaden and Bishop are trying to add another gray hair to my head. How hard can it be to find a receptionist?" I grumbled, more to myself than to her.

Jaden's voice echoed from the doorway. "Boss. Aimee. Food? I love you even more," he said, his eyes lighting up at the sight of the pastries.

Aimee moved to the side table, setting down the box beside the coffee, teas, and other beverages. My eyes followed her, lingering on the way she moved, the way her hair was pulled into a high ponytail, baring the delicate curve of her neck. The sight was enough to send a rush of warmth through me, a reminder of how deeply I cared for this woman. But before I could dwell on it, Jaden cleared his throat, snapping me back to the present.

"Boss, I'm going to meet the Anson team," he said, but my attention remained on Aimee as she carefully transferred the pastries to a platter.

Watching her like some lovesick puppy and not a grown man, I knew deep down in my bones, it was time. I needed to make a visit, one that I never imagined making.

Fifty-Eight

Aimee

Between running the Blue Orchid line and preparing for the upcoming opening of the Anson Resort, now less than five weeks away, my mind constantly buzzed with things that needed to be done. The thought of returning to the duplex loomed in the background, but I wasn't ready—not yet, maybe not ever. I longed for a sense of independence again. After a long discussion with Dr. Taitt and a quiet conversation with Drago, we reached an agreement. Bishop had no immediate plans to visit, so I moved into his condo. Jaden and Tanisha were my neighbors, and Drago was upstairs. Sebastian lived with me. I guess I really was a cat stealer.

The door chimed softly, and as always, Drago waited for my acknowledgment before stepping inside. My gaze swept over him—those black jeans hugged his frame perfectly. The black shirt with sleeves rolled up revealed his strong forearms. His presence had a way of grounding me.

"Aimee? Aimee!" Topaz called at me through the phone.

"Sorry. I got distracted," I admitted, shaking myself from the trance he so effortlessly put me in.

Topaz's laughter bubbled through the phone, warm and teasing. "I bet you did. Tell Drago hello for me. Anyway, I'll update the project plan so everyone knows that all the beds and linens have arrived and will be delivered tomorrow."

"Leila and I will finalize the RSVPs, so we'll have a headcount of our guests."

"This is really happening," she said, her voice carrying a mix of excitement and disbelief.

"Yup. Don't get too excited and disturb my nephew." The thought of what could have happened—what that psycho almost destroyed—made my chest tighten. I wasn't sure I could have survived if he had succeeded in ruining Topaz's dreams.

"Research says you should stimulate babies when they're in the womb. This is good stimulation. Anyway, enjoy, and all the best with your conversation."

At the mention of the discussion I'd been dodging for weeks, my pulse quickened. I couldn't avoid it anymore. Drago crossed the room, closing the distance between us in a few strides. I reached up, wrapping my hands around his neck, pulling him in for a kiss. His lips found mine, warm and familiar, and when he gently nibbled my lower lip, it sent a shiver down my spine.

"If you kiss me like that again, we'll be late for our reservation. To save time, we'll take the chopper over," he said, his voice low and teasing, though his eyes held a deeper promise.

I grabbed my bag, and we left. Inviting Drago to dinner to have this conversation seemed like a good idea at the time—Fish Pot was remote and beautiful, a place I hadn't visited in a while. It was perfect, or at least it had been in my mind. But now, doubt crept in. I was being a chicken, plain and simple.

Drago helped me into the chopper, his hand steadying me as I climbed in. Once we were airborne, the landscape of Etim spread out beneath us, the sun high and bright, casting everything in a golden glow. The closer we got to Fish Pot, the more the world seemed to shimmer—the boats bobbing on the waves, the water sparkling like a thousand diamonds. It was a scene straight out of a dream, but reality weighed heavily on my chest.

Once we arrived, Drago kept his hand in mine as we made our way to the restaurant. I requested a secluded section, away from the evening crowd that would soon fill the place. Drago pulled out my chair, a small gesture that made my heart ache with the deep care I felt for him. The host presented the menu options, and I barely registered the words. I let Drago take charge, trusting him to choose while my thoughts spun, tangled in the conversation we were about to have.

When the host left, Drago turned to me, a teasing glint in his eye. "Don't tell me you brought me all the way out here to dump me?"

The server arrived with sparkling water, which Drago opened and poured with the same calm precision he brought to everything. I took a sip, the coolness grounding me for what was to come. Breathing deeply, I locked eyes with Drago. He studied me with that intense focus he reserved for solving the most complex problems. "Dr. Taitt referred me to a specialist," I began, the words tasting foreign on my tongue.

His brows drew together, casting a shadow over the warmth in his gaze. The slight downturn of his lips, the way his eyes held mine without blinking—he was trying to piece it all together, to understand what this meant.

"I'm not dying. At least not yet," I said, trying to lighten the mood, though the joke fell flat. But by the end of tonight, if I died, my death certificate would read, 'Death by Embarrassment'

"I didn't think you were dying," he said, his voice calm, though his eyes hadn't lost their intensity. "But based on my interactions with Dr. Taitt and my research, she's one of the leading experts in her field."

As the server placed the vegetable and fish spring rolls on the table, I smoothed my napkin over my lap, hoping the action would help calm my nerves.

"Not in this area," I clarified as Drago placed two spring rolls on each of our plates.

"I've never..." I lowered my voice to a whisper. "Been...been intimate." I dropped my eyes from his briefly then forced myself to make eye contact once more. "Like...sex. Like had—" My cheeks burned from the embarrassment of this conversation. His face remained steady on mine. I rushed my words to get it all over with, "She referred me to a sex therapist."

Drago continued eating, taking a measured sip of his wine. On my end, a burst of sweat tried to test the claim, yet again, that my makeup foundation was a hundred percent waterproof.

I pressed on. "Being honest, I don't know how I'll respond to being touched, to even having sex. We've held hands, kissed on the cheek, even on the lips. But outside of Hartwell Manor, everything has been PG. The truth is, I don't know. I've never had a man's hand on my skin, on my body, unless it was for an advertising campaign."

I took a sip of my wine, trying to steady the tremor in my hands. Drago moved his chair closer to mine, his hazel eyes softening as he reached out to take my hand. His touch was gentle, reassuring, and it gave me the strength to voice the fears I'd kept buried for so long. "I want a family, a husband. I want it all. But before..." I hesitated, my breath hitching as I tried to push the words out. "Before, I couldn't tolerate any of it. What if, now, I can't ever bear to be touched in that way, even by you?"

Fifty-Nine

Drago

Aimee's fingers flicked through the channels with casual disinterest. Tonight's conversation still pinged in my mind, a mix of admiration and awe at her willingness to confront her deepest fears head-on. She was braver than she gave herself credit for. Propped against the arm of the sofa, she kept shifting her position, the remote loose in her grip, as if no angle could ease the tension from our earlier words.

I went to the kitchen and returned with two unopened bottles of sparkling water. I handed one to her, and as I was about to go back to the kitchen to get the glasses, she held my arm and looked at me, her eyes steady and clear. "Know that I trust you. You don't have to give me bottles that are unopened." The words were simple, yet they held a depth that struck me straight in the chest. *I trust you*—it was something priceless and hearing it from her lips meant more than anything money could buy.

"What are we watching?" I asked, hoping to shift the mood to something lighter.

"Let's pick something from the nineties. *The Matrix? Pretty Woman?*" Her tone was playful, a hint of challenge in her voice.

"*The Matrix*," I suggested.

"*Pretty Woman*," she responded, her lips curling into a small, teasing smile.

I set my glass down on the table, a plan forming in my mind. "Sit forward. I'm going to slide in behind you." She obliged, and as I moved closer, the warmth of her body against mine brought a sense of contentment. Except for our shoes, we were still fully dressed—she in her chocolate-brown pants and cream, off-the-shoulder top. That style was part of her signature look—or at least one she clearly preferred.

Settling in behind her, I said, "Now rest on my chest."

"Is this your effort to get me comfortable with touching?" Her voice was light, but the underlying vulnerability was unmistakable.

Reaching for my water, I replied, "The movie is starting."

She placed her glass on the floor, and a small pang of worry tugged at me—she might get up and forget it and end up cutting her foot. I rose and took both glasses to the kitchen, then slid behind her again. The sensation of her body nestled against mine was pure bliss. I smoothed my hand over her hair, pressing a gentle kiss to the top of her head. It was a simple gesture, but it carried the weight of my unspoken emotions, everything I hadn't yet put into words.

Before Vivian even made it to Rodeo Drive in the movie, I heard the telltale signs of Aimee falling asleep—the soft, rhythmic breaths that signaled she had drifted off. She shifted in her sleep, body relaxing more heavily against mine, the movement causing her to brush against me in a way that sparked a fire I wasn't prepared to deal with.

Reaching for the remote, I needed to redirect my thoughts, and fast. Her trust was something I valued too much to let my mind wander where it shouldn't. With a quick press of the button, I switched to *The Matrix*, hoping the action would help focus my mind on something other than the woman laying on my chest.

Sixty

Drago

My coat flared out behind me, the collar turned up against the biting Boston autumn wind that cut through the city like a whip. The air carried the sharp, crisp edge of late October, tinged with the scent of fallen leaves and the first hints of winter. It had been a relentless few months, the kind where days blurred into nights and every hour was accounted for. But with the grand opening of the resort looming tomorrow, I couldn't delay this trip any longer.

Since the night Aimee opened up to me, a new rhythm had settled between us. Every evening became our time when we would do something together—lay on the couch, where she inevitably fell asleep on my chest halfway through a movie; go for walks and link our hands; or even cook together. We'd started going to the pool after our workouts. A smile tugged at the corners of my mouth as I remembered the way she would try to dunk me, that playful glint in her eye as she thought she'd caught me off guard by jumping on my back. I'd let myself sink under the water, letting her think she'd won. It wasn't about winning or losing; it was about helping her find comfort with me, building that safe space brick by brick.

We hadn't spent a day apart, not until last night. The final preparations for the resort's soft opening demanded all our attention. Topaz, Shae, Aimee, and the entire planning team had been there two days prior to the arrival of our family and friends to make sure everything was perfect for them. Our friends and family enjoyed the amenities, their laughter and conversations filled the spaces that Topaz and her team created. But now, with everything set for tomorrow's grand opening, there was somewhere else I needed to be.

My steps carried me closer, down the familiar path. There was a peaceful calmness that enveloped the evening, a hush that only descended as the world began to quiet. The grass underfoot was soft, slightly damp from an earlier drizzle of rain, and the air around me grew heavier as I approached the spot I last visited two years ago. The fresh flowers that I arranged to be delivered every week marked the place I avoided, hoping to lessen my pain.

I crouched down, my fingers brushing over the cool metal of the plaque. The words engraved there were as permanent as the loss they represented: *My beautiful, loving wife, Minerva Baas, the light of my soul*. "Sorry I didn't come before," I began, my voice low, almost swallowed by the evening breeze. "But it was difficult." Tears gathered at the corners of my eyes, blurring the lines of the inscription. "When I moved to Etim, it was to escape the memories of us in this city. I missed you so much, Minerva. I needed to move on, and I couldn't do it here."

The tombstone was smooth beneath my hand, a tangible connection to a life that was no more. "I lied," I admitted, the words catching in my throat. "I promised at your funeral, as they lowered you into the ground, that you would always be the love of my life. But I met someone, and I've fallen in love with her. I thought you and I would have grown old together... but that didn't happen. Maybe I might grow old with her."

Tears slipped down my cheeks, each one carrying a piece of the grief I'd held onto for so long. "Her name is Aimee Patel. She's nothing like you. You might not have picked her for me in a million years—or maybe you would have. She's loving, strong, brave. My loving her doesn't mean I've stopped loving you. I loved our time together, and I wanted you to know about her."

Reaching into my pocket, I pulled out a small object, turning it over in my hand before holding it up as if showing it to her. "You had better taste than me. I think she'll like this. Not your style, but I've come to know her over the last six months... Maybe you had a hand in it. After all, it was because of Winter—who's married now, by the way—that we got together. Trust your sister to hold the wedding at a couples-only resort."

A rustle and the soft thud of footsteps on the grass signaled someone's approach. A hand came to rest on my shoulder, a gentle but firm touch. "She would want you to be happy," Reverend Veronica said, her voice clear and decisive.

I rose to my feet, turning to face her. Reverend Vee was just as I remembered—tall, with that commanding presence softened by the kindness in her blue eyes. I used to tease Minerva that her pastor must have Viking roots, a joke that always earned me a fond eye roll from both women.

"I'm glad you called," she said, her tone warm and steady. "Minerva and your love were pure. When someone loves you, they want you to be happy. Moving on doesn't mean you love Minerva any less. She will forever hold a special place in your heart."

Returning her hand to rest on my shoulder, she said, "Let me pray for you." She bowed her head, and I did the same, letting her words wash over me. After she finished, she patted my shoulder gently, her eyes full of understanding. "Follow your heart, Drago. God has blessed you with a second chance. Grasp it and don't let it go."

Sixty-One

Aimee

"Look up toward the ceiling. Eyeliner, and we're done. Keep still. Nothing will fall apart. We've got this."

Topaz was a ball of nerves. She shook more than a bag of snakes. The last thing I needed was to accidentally poke her in her eye as I applied her makeup.

"Sara Anson and Queen Candace will arrive in two hours, Aimee, two hours," she reminded me, as if time itself needed to be kept in check.

"All done."

Shae entered the room and said, "Not quite." His tux was perfectly tailored, accentuating his broad shoulders and confident stride. But it was the way his eyes never strayed from his wife that caught my attention. He crossed the room in a few easy steps, stopping behind her. From the velvet-lined box in his hand, he drew out a necklace—a stunning cascade of diamonds and topaz. The jewels glistened as he carefully fastened the necklace around her neck.

"This completes your outfit," he said as he pulled out the matching earrings. "I want you to treasure this day. You worked hard for it. I love you."

Their eyes met in the mirror, a silent conversation passing between them that spoke of their love, support, and shared dreams.

"Don't cry! That mascara and eyeliner will run. I'll cry for you," I said, trying to keep my own voice steady as tears pricked at the corners of my eyes.

Topaz stood, the gown flowing gracefully around her as she turned to hug her husband. There was something so right about this moment, as if everything had come full circle. After she and Shae shared their embrace, I stepped in, gently adjusting the delicate fabric of her dress, the one she entrusted me to design. My hands moved over the intricate embroidery that cascaded down the front of the gown, feeling the fine threads and the way the silver satin shimmered under the lights. The deep blue accents woven into the fabric complemented the jewelry Shae had just given her, tying everything together in a perfect blend of elegance and grace. The gown draped effortlessly over her growing belly.

I left them to their moment and walked to my adjoining room. We were staying in the princess suites, a luxurious space that exuded opulence at every turn. Across from my room were the prince suites where Drago was staying. I pulled some strings to add Tanisha to the guest list—a small token of apology for taking one of her precious vials, which I used on Kiran Ramdas. Tanisha had figured it out, of course. She was too sharp not to. But she wasn't concerned. She knew, without question, that the vial had not been intended for Drago.

Topaz and I settled on a silver theme for our dresses, a decision that had been easy in the end. Her gown was meant to be a showstopper, a piece that would leave everyone breathless. Mine, by contrast, was more understated, a nod to classic Hollywood 1990s red carpet style. I traced my fingers over the fabric, feeling the smoothness under my fingertips as I glanced at the clock. Drago promised he would return in time for the grand opening, and whatever had taken him away had to be significant. The days had been packed, every moment filled with the final preparations. Yesterday was a whirlwind, coordinating with the kitchen and restaurant staff for the dinner that would follow the opening. Even in the chaos, I missed him. His absence was ever present, even when I collapsed in bed exhausted last night. Or rather this morning.

I paused at the double vanity, the cool marble beneath my palms, as I set out my makeup. I had already showered, the warm water easing some of the tension from my muscles before I went to help Topaz. Now, it was time to focus on myself.

As I removed my dress and stood before the mirror, I replayed my last conversation with Dr. Hayes in my mind. The thoughts swirled, a mix of apprehension and longing. I wanted Drago to touch me—not in the casual ways we had before, the hand-holding, the kisses on the cheek. But not sex… I was nowhere near ready for sex. I wanted to see how I would respond to his touch in an intimate, deliberate way. Dr. Hayes, with her calm, measured advice, never pushed her beliefs on me, though she had shared them. As a Christian sex therapist, she wasn't an advocate for premarital sex, so she offered ways to explore intimacy without crossing that line.

I wanted to try. The only way to do it was to ask Drago. But with all our clothes on. The more I thought about it, the more the idea seemed to waver between possibility and doubt. Drago never pressured me, not once. Pausing with the blush brush in my hand, I laughed softly at the realization. We had been touching all this time—watching movies, holding hands, playing in the pool. It had all been so innocent, yet not once had I been repulsed by him. Drago had always been a source of comfort, never a cause for fear.

Tonight. Yes. Tonight, I was going to test how comfortable I was, to see how far I'd come. Finishing my makeup, I slipped into my gown. It hugged my figure like a second skin, the shimmering silver fabric catching the light with every step I took. The off-the-shoulder neckline draped elegantly across my collarbones, adding a touch of understated glamour. The fabric gathered at the waist, accentuating my curves, with a slit along my left leg that showed off my newly acquired and toned muscles when I walked.

The evening unfolded as I mingled with guests, a glass of white wine in my hand as I moved through the crowd. A hand slipped into the crook of my elbow, and I looked down to see dark eyes smiling up at me. Tanisha beamed with delight, her excitement contagious. "My room is wicked," she said, her voice filled with enthusiasm. "I have plenty more vials at home. Come and help yourself to them if I get to stay here again."

"That might give both Drago and Jaden undue stress," I replied with a chuckle. "Where's Jaden?"

Tanisha pointed to the other side of the room, where Jaden and Leila were deep in conversation. "They look like they are plotting to overtake the world."

With a smile, she said, "Oh yeah. They definitely have something up their sleeves."

Topaz signaled to me. "I'm going over to Topaz. We're starting soon."

I wove my way through the guests and servers toward Topaz, scanning the crowd as I walked. On reaching Topaz, we stood and talked until she was notified of the arrival of Queen Candace and her entourage. The Ansons, including Topaz, went to greet the Queen. The national anthem of Etim played to announce her arrival. Jordan broke away from the group when the anthem was finished, his easy smile widening as he approached me.

He pulled me into a warm embrace. His presence was always a comfort. "How are you doing?" he asked, his voice low and sincere.

"I'm good," I replied, lifting my gaze to meet his. "Thank you for everything."

"If I weren't commitment averse, I'd steal you away from Drago. He's good for you."

Smiling at him, I teased, "Someday, Jordan, the right woman will come along."

"She hasn't been born yet," he quipped with a grin. "That means by the time she's old enough to marry, some of my parts might not be working. Or I'll be dead."

"One of these days, Jordan, I'll be in the front seat. Well, not the front seat—it would be a royal wedding. I'd be in row twenty or twenty-one of Etim Cathedral." He laughed, his rich voice drawing a few glances our way. He placed a kiss on my cheek before moving on. I continued scanning the room, my thoughts drifting to Drago. Where is he? Lord, I hope all is well.

As if sensing my thoughts, Topaz appeared beside me, her hand slipping into mine as she muttered, "Don't worry, all will be well."

The orchestra played, filling the air with a melody that seemed to carry the promise of the evening. Food flowed freely, guests mingled, and glasses clinked in celebration. Soon, Sara and Shawn Anson would officially cut the ribbon, declaring the opening of Needham's Point Anson Resort. My heart thudded in my chest with anticipation—I didn't want Drago to miss it.

Topaz's grip on my hand tightened slightly, and when I followed her gaze, there he was. A smile spread across her face as she whispered, "Told you all would be well."

Yes, all was well in my world as Drago made his way toward me. His hazel eyes roamed my face, and when our eyes locked, there was a look there that sent a cascade of tingles through me, something new and electrifying. For some strange reason, I welcomed every one of them.

Yes, tonight. Drago's touch...tonight.

Sixty-Two

Drago

Aimee's head rested on my shoulder as we walked to her room. She wore a different fragrance tonight—bolder than her usual powdery sweet scent, with subtle jasmine undertones. Each step brought us nearer to her door, but all I could think about was the way her body fit perfectly against mine. The silk of her dress whispered against my arm, and I envied every thread that got to caress her skin.

The moment I saw her tonight, something inside me snapped. Heat surged through my veins, an uncontrollable force that gripped my spine and sent shivers to every nerve. My pulse pounded in my ears, a relentless rhythm drowned out everything but the sight of her. The dress traced every line of her figure, leaving my mouth dry and my thoughts scattered. As she moved, the slit in her gown revealed just enough of her leg to drive me wild, the delicate line of her calf teasing with each graceful step as she mingled with the guests.

It was absurd—over the past few months, we'd run together. I'd seen her in athletic gear, even swimwear, but tonight was different. Tonight, she was a vision of raw, unfiltered allure. She screamed provocative. Sexy.

As we approached the elevator that went directly to her room, the drumming in my ear returned, this time louder. It was as if I was at a rock concert and the drummer was doing a solo performance. The polished doors reflected her figure beside me. My hand trembled slightly as I swiped her card, allowing the elevator to ascend. Not even when my life was on the line on a mission had my hands shook anywhere near like this.

She leaned into me, her breath warm against my neck. "Magical," she whispered, her voice laced with a soft, contented sigh. The sound sent a jolt through me, causing me to tighten my grip on the card. "Seeing it unfold. I'm so proud of Topaz. I enjoyed this more than my launch."

"You did?" My voice barely masked the tremor beneath it.

"Yes. This is amazing. Friends are the family you get to choose. I saw that somewhere, but it's so true. I couldn't have a better sister than Topaz. I'm happy for her."

I pressed a kiss to the top of her head, lingering longer than necessary, drawing in the warmth she exuded. When she lifted her head, her lips brushed against mine, a featherlight touch that nearly undid me. The elevator doors opened, but the lights remained dim, the usual glow replaced by something softer, more intimate.

"Why didn't the lights come on? Oh, no. The last thing we need is an electrical problem." Her voice carried a hint of concern, but then her eyes caught the soft flicker of candles scattered throughout the room. "Candles...beautiful. Topaz kept this surprise from me."

I couldn't help but laugh, the sound low and rough as I glanced down at her. "She definitely kept it a secret from you." The flames danced in the reflection of the windows, casting shadows that flickered like whispers of what was to come. I led her onto the balcony, where torches flared softly, the glow of the firelight mingling with the distant crash of waves below. The ocean was a dark, endless expanse, mirroring the midnight sky that stretched above us.

Taking her left hand, I turned her to face me. "Topaz kept this a secret because it was my secret to tell."

Her eyes locked onto mine, the unshed tears in them catching the light like tiny stars. I said to her in a low tone, "You were an intrusion in my life, one I did not expect, one I needed, one I didn't even know I needed."

A single tear slipped free, trailing down her cheek. I caught it with my thumb, then brought the drop to my lips, tasting the salt and the emotion she couldn't contain. "Aimee, I want you in all my nows. I want you in all my tomorrows. I want you in my forevers. I love you with my entire being."

I released her hand only long enough to retrieve the small black pouch from my jacket pocket. The weight of what was inside was nothing compared to the gravity of this moment. I drew out the ring, the oval-cut Kashmir sapphire catching the light and glowing like the night itself. The Argyle pink diamonds that surrounded it sparkled with a fire all their own, each one flawless, rare, but could not compare to her.

Taking her left hand, I asked, "Will you marry me? So I can have all your forevers?"

Her nod was immediate, fervent, as if the words couldn't come fast enough. "Yes. Yes! I so love you, Drago."

I slipped the ring into place. Then I pulled her close, my mouth capturing hers in a kiss that was both a promise and a possession. My tongue traced the curve of her lips, delving deeper, drawing her tight against me until there was no space left between us.

A burst of explosions outside startled her, and she jerked back from me.

The second fireworks displayed went off, with the words, "She Said Yes."

Tears ran down her face. She reached up and touched my face. "I want you to do something for me."

Kissing her, I responded, "For you, anything."

Sixty-Three

Aimee

My smile should have been dazzling. A radiant match for the ring Drago had just slipped onto my finger. But as we walked toward the bedroom, our fingers intertwined, the voice in my head grew louder, each word echoing like a drumbeat of doubt. *What do you think you're doing? You're not normal. His hands will crawl your skin, and you'll throw up all over him. Nice going—engaged for a full ten minutes before he calls it off.*

The words stung like a slap, but they weren't new. They'd been lurking, waiting for this moment to strike, to remind me of all the reasons I believed I wasn't good enough. The other part of my brain seemed to have left the building, offering no encouragement, no reassuring words—*nothing*.

We reached the threshold of the bedroom, and I stopped, unable to force my feet over the line that separated the living room from the space where everything might change. I tilted my head up, meeting Drago's gaze, my heart pounding so loudly I wondered if he could hear it. Desire and anxiety collided within me, each vying for dominance as our lips brushed in a tentative kiss. The warmth of his breath mingled with mine.

He paused, his eyes searching mine with a tenderness that nearly unraveled me. "What is it you want?" he asked, his voice gentle, almost a caress.

I glanced past him to the bed. I wasn't sure I could make the step. But I had to push forward. We had gotten engaged; it wasn't about the ring—this was about our future. And that future would include this. My mind raced, but I pushed the doubts aside. *You. Can. Do. This.*

With our hands still linked, I took a step forward, then another, crossing into the bedroom. The world didn't stop; it kept spinning, and the voices in my head grew quieter, retreating into the background as I focused on Drago. We approached the bed, and I halted, turning to face him. My hands trembled slightly as I reached for the buttons of his jacket, slipping each one free with deliberate care. The fabric was soft under my fingers as I helped him out of it, and I placed it neatly on the bench at the foot of the bed.

I kicked off my shoes, the carpet soft against my bare feet, and watched as Drago did the same, his movements unhurried, as if he was giving me all the time I needed. His eyes never left my face, his expression open, patient. I climbed onto the bed first, settling myself on the plush covers. He followed. A swirl of emotions threatened to overwhelm me.

"Lie beside me, facing me," I said, my voice steadier than I expected.

"We don't have to—" he began, his concern evident in the way he held himself back.

Scooting closer until our bodies were just inches apart, I said, "Kiss me. Don't hold back."

He threaded his fingers through my hair, slowly, deliberately, sending shivers down my spine. "What are you comfortable with?" he asked, his tone soft, almost reverent.

"This," I replied, swallowing the lump in my throat. "Baby steps. I don't think I'm ready for you to be on top of me."

His response was wordless. His lips found the curve of my jaw and traced a path down to the neckline of my dress. His kisses were gentle, testing, as though he was reading my reactions with every touch. His hand slipped to my waist, pulling me closer, until our bodies were pressed together. Lying on our sides, fully clothed, I could feel the heat of him, the undeniable evidence of his erection pressing into me as his mouth found mine, devouring it in a way that made my toes curl. A moan escaped. Happiness replaced the trepidation from moments ago.

Baby steps.

Baby steps—and it was so good.

Sixty-Four

Drago

A tremble traveled through Aimee's foot, a silent signal of her nervousness, which stilled under the weight of my hand.

The screen blinked, stating the host had joined the meeting.

Dr. Hayes appeared on screen, her glasses perched atop her head, her smile controlled, the corners of her lips lifted enough to create soft lines that hinted at kindness.

"Hello, Drago. A pleasure to meet you, finally."

Nodding, with my hand resting on Aimee's thigh, I replied, "Same here."

Glancing at the file before her, she asked, "Set a date for the wedding?"

"In five months," Aimee said at the same time as I said, "April."

"It seems somebody is counting down to the wedding?"

Aimee moved her chair closer to mine and held my hands. "Dr. Hayes, I mentioned wanting to have a few sessions with Drago as we prepare for our wedding and our life together."

Leaning forward, she continued, "Have you spoken about—?"

Color bloomed across Aimee's golden complexion. "No." I said. "However, we've continued to explore touching, but only fully clothed." Glancing at Aimee, I said, "We've agreed to wait until marriage."

A smile took over her face. "I'm so glad when my clients make that decision." Turning to Aimee, she asked, "Have you shared your fears with Drago?"

"Fears?" I asked with a raised brow.

"About sex. You know...before... I can't—."

Leaning toward her and capturing her lips, I assured her, "Trust me. We won't have a problem."

A throat cleared. "I'm still here," Dr. Hayes said, with a hint of a smile in her voice.

We spent about fifteen minutes discussing how women respond to their trauma in different ways. Focusing on Aimee, she said, "In a previous session, we explored some possible sexual positions that Aimee might feel safe to explore initially, in the early phase of your marriage. Aimee, do you want to share?"

I squeezed her hand and brought it to my lips to encourage her.

Her cheeks darkened with a visible blush, as she responded, "I think any position where I'm on top, on the side or you're beh—just not you on top. At least not right now." Biting her lip, she added, "But that could change."

Dr. Hayes encouraged us to continue exploring touch in safe ways, given our position of waiting until marriage.

Ending the call, I lifted her onto me and asked, "So, you want to be in control?"

Running her hands through my hair and leaning forward, she replied softly, "Something like that."

The little imp rocked against me, causing a moan to escape from my lips.

Sixty-Five

Aimee

"Jaden, it's obvious you wish me to die at the hands of my soon-to-be wife," Drago said, his tone a mix of amusement and mock exasperation.

I knocked lightly before stepping into the room, catching the playful tension in the air. "Now, why would I want to kill you?" I teased, flashing a grin at Jaden. "Hi, Jaden." I made my way to Drago's chair, leaning in to brush my lips against his for a quick, affectionate kiss.

Drago's eyes never left Jaden as he pointed at him, a slight smirk tugging at the corner of his mouth. "You tell her. Not me."

I raised a brow. "Tell me what?"

Jaden straightened, as if bracing for my reaction. "Leila isn't taking another contract with the military. Given her training, I think she'd be the perfect addition to our team—administrative assistant plus surveillance work."

My mind processed the information quickly. "I'm not going to kill you," I said, more amused than anything. "Leila will work for me on weekends and with you full time. We already talked about it. I'm in production mode, and I could use my virtual assistant service."

Jaden shot Drago a pointed look, as if to say, *I told you so.* "I told you, if you gave me time, I'd find the perfect receptionist. Well, I've upgraded the position and pay."

A small laugh escaped me as I added, "She's not broke, either. Jordan let her keep the money from Ramdas."

Jaden, sensing his need to escape, took a step toward the door. "I'll set up a meeting for her with Bishop. I don't think he'll mind," he offered, his tone light as he slipped out of the room, leaving Drago and me alone.

As the door clicked shut behind him, "Ready to go collect our rings?" I asked, unable to keep the smile from spreading across my face. The thought of those rings, a symbol of everything we'd been through and everything that lay ahead, made my heart race. "I can't believe, in two weeks, we'll be married."

Drago's eyes softened, his gaze steady and full of promise. He reached for my hand, his fingers threading through mine. We turned toward the door, ready to step into the next chapter of our lives.

Sixty-Six

Drago

The wedding planning had been as smooth as we could have hoped, thanks to the meticulous event planners at Anson's Resort. They handled every detail, allowing us to spend time with Dr. Taitt and Dr. Hayes. Reverend Veronica did our pre-marital counseling.

We wanted a small, intimate wedding, but as it turned out, our definition of "small" ended up being one hundred and fifty people. Among them were my parents, who flew in a week before the wedding so they could spend time with us. Also, Luna, Winter, and her husband. Bishop stood beside me, his presence a quiet pillar of strength. "Drago, you deserve this happiness," he said, his voice low, carrying the weight of years of friendship and understanding.

"We all do," I replied, my gaze steady on the scene before us.

Bishop's lips curved into a bittersweet smile. "Some of us didn't get the happily ever after gene."

The music shifted, and the instrumental notes filled the room, signaling the start of something beautiful. Topaz entered, her cream, floor-length dress moving gracefully with each step. An orchid wrist corsage added the finishing touch to her outfit. Aimee—*my wife*, the words echoing in my mind with a sense of wonder—designed both of their dresses. The thought brought a sense of pride, knowing her creativity touched this moment in such a profound way.

The first notes of the cello began, and the pastor's voice gently instructed everyone to stand. I wanted to keep my focus forward, to steady myself for the moment to come, but something pulled me, an irresistible force that turned my head to the back of the room. There she was, Aimee, walking up the aisle, her arm linked with Crown Prince Jordan's. He, in his ever-protective manner, had taken on the role of her self-appointed big brother.

She was a vision. Her off-the-shoulder dress shimmered with thousands of Swarovski crystals, each catching the evening sun that streamed through the open doors of the circular conference room. The light danced across the fabric, making her appear almost ethereal, as if she had stepped out of a dream. The train of her gown flowed behind her like a river of silver, every movement deliberate, every step filled with purpose. She was stunning, breathtaking, and she was walking toward me, ready to become mine forever.

Aimee's smile was radiant, her eyes locked onto mine, communicating everything we had been through, everything we were about to become. As she reached the altar, Topaz stepped forward, gently taking the blue orchids from Aimee's hands. With a graceful movement, Aimee's hand slipped into mine, her touch warm and reassuring. The pastor began the ceremony, his voice a steady backdrop to the emotions swirling around us.

When the pastor asked who gives this woman in marriage, Jordan leaned in close, his voice firm but carrying a hint of affection. "Treat her well, Drago. You don't want to make an enemy out of me."

I met his gaze, the seriousness of the moment reflected in his eyes. "I will. You have my word."

As the clergyman declared us husband and wife, the room seemed to pause, the air thick with anticipation. "You may kiss the bride," he said, the words both an invitation and a command. I didn't hesitate. My hands found Aimee's waist, pulling her gently but firmly toward me. Her hair, pinned up in an intricate style, remained undisturbed as I lowered my lips to hers. The kiss was anything but chaste.

Aimee was mine, and I was hers. Forever.

Aimee

Drago scooped me up with ease, carrying me over the threshold as if I weighed nothing. The warmth of his arms around me was a comforting contrast to the cool evening air that lingered outside. Topaz and Shae gifted us a week at the resort, the luxurious Queen Candace suite awaiting us—a sanctuary after the whirlwind of the day.

As he set me down gently, I took a moment to soak in the beauty of the evening, the glow of the moonlight streaming through the open windows, casting a soft, delicate light across the room. "Drago, it was a beautiful evening," I began, my voice low with the emotion that had been building all day. "I'm so glad I found you. Thank you for being my husband; I will treasure you always. Our journey to get here wasn't easy, and I know the future will have its ups and downs, but remember that I love and treasure you."

He leaned down, his breath warm against my cheek as I tilted my head up, our eyes locking in a moment of shared understanding. Without hesitation, I wrapped my arms around him, pulling him close. Our kiss started slow, a tender connection that quickly deepened, becoming something more urgent, more intense. Our lips moved together in perfect harmony, and for a moment, everything else faded away.

When I finally pulled back, breathless but unwilling to break the connection completely, I smiled up at him. "Before you distract me any further, I have a gift for you. Or rather, for us." With a playful grin, I slipped out of his embrace and disappeared into the room, returning a moment later with a square box wrapped in simple, elegant paper. I held it out to him. He took it from me and shook it. Teasing, I said, "It's not for shaking. Open it."

Drago's curiosity was evident as he tore off the wrapping paper. He lifted the lid, pushed aside the tissue paper, and then chuckled as he pulled out the contents, holding them up for us both to see.

"His and hers boxing gloves," he said, a grin spreading across his face as he examined the gloves more closely.

"With the date of our wedding embroidered on the cuffs," I added, pointing to the neat stitching that marked the moment we became husband and wife.

Drago's grin widened, a mischievous glint in his eyes. "I have something for us too, but we'll explore that in bed."

"Sir, you're sounding a little spicy there," I teased, my heart racing in anticipation of what was to come.

Without another word, Drago pulled me back into his arms, his movements deliberate yet filled with a sense of urgency. He turned me around, his fingers deftly working to unfasten the delicate buttons of my dress. As the fabric slipped from my shoulders, pooling at my feet, I reached down to remove my shoes, but his hand on mine stopped me.

"Leave them on," he murmured, his voice a low rumble that sent a shiver of excitement through me.

I met his gaze, the intensity in his eyes making my pulse quicken. "Come here and undress me." His voice was a soft but firm invitation that I didn't want to refuse.

"With pleasure."

Epilogue

Aimee

Seven Months Later

"Where are we going?"

Leaning over, I kissed Drago's cheek. "Stop pouting. It's a surprise."

"You know it's my birthday celebration, and I hate surprises."

The captain welcomed us aboard and announced our travel time would be two and a half hours. Drago glanced over at me. "So, we're not going that far?"

"Kiss me, because that's the only thing you're getting from these lips."

Drago placed a series of soft kisses across my lips before slipping his tongue into my mouth. He groaned as he pulled away.

"I better stop before we join the Mile High Club. Not that I'm opposed to it."

I ran my hand up his thigh, arching a brow at him until I found him hard against my hand.

"You wicked wife."

I removed my hand and rested my head on his shoulder. The hostess moved around, preparing a light snack, as we would have dinner when we landed. This trip had taken four months of intense sessions with both Dr. Taitt and Dr. Hayes. Those Bible verses about transforming your mind and thoughts—I'd read that book about five times, and I believed I could quote some of it by heart. I threw everything into preparing for this. This was as much a gift to me as it was to Drago.

The flight attendant served us chicken liver pâté with toasted baguette slices and crackers, along with miniature bottles of water and wine. Forty minutes after our plates were cleared, the captain announced to prepare for landing, that we would be on the ground in ten minutes.

Drago cocked his head at me. I pretended to zip my mouth, and he laughed. As the plane touched down, I prayed and declared, "I'm whole. Healed. Emotionally healed."

Drago held my hand, and when I opened my eyes, I found him watching me. His brows knitted together, lines deepening around his eyes. I smiled at him as the captain announced, "Happy Birthday, Mr. Baas, and welcome to Paris."

Drago gripped my hand a little tighter. I trailed my finger along his face. "I'm good. We're good."

The driver took us to our hotel. I selected this one because, for me, nothing was more iconic or representative of Paris than the Eiffel Tower. Every room, except for the bathroom, offered a view of the iconic monument.

We dined in our room with the drapes open, revealing the Eiffel Tower in all its glory. Drago, sensing this was a pivotal moment in my healing process, moved his table setting next to mine.

We gazed through the window as we ate. Then I placed my fork down and solemnly said to my husband, "A few months ago, I thought about what I wanted to do for your birthday."

"You didn't need to—"

Shaking my head, I interrupted, "Wrong. I needed to face my demons so we can have an even richer future. This is as much for me as it is for you." Locking eyes with him, I said, "You see, I want it all with you." Closing my eyes and taking a deep breath, I added, "I mean all."

Standing, I said, "Give me two minutes." I walked to the bedroom and returned with a box and presented it to him. "Open it in three minutes and then join me." I placed a kiss on his lips and returned to the bedroom.

I slipped off my dress, which I had put on two hours ago, after we enjoyed a leisurely bath together. I left on the lacy, barely-there lingerie, which was held together by three ribbons. Drago walked into the room with the box, holding the tie which he had removed from it.

"Tonight, you're fully in control. I want to feel your weight on me." The words came out easier than I thought. As he slowly unbuttoned his shirt, I slid backwards onto the bed admiring the contours of his muscles. Almost panther like, he moved toward the bed and removed his pants before joining me in bed.

He worshipped my body with kisses, and he undid the tiny bows holding together my last remaining piece of clothing, if you can call it that. This was a hot seller from my line, and I saw why. Removing his boxers, he lowered his body on top of me, warm and comforting. Not suffocating. I welcomed it.

Lifting my eyes to meet his, I wrapped my legs around him. Tapping me on my nose, he said, "I'm in control." Smiling devilishly, he added, "And I have the entire night to play. After all, you gave all sorts of toys, including handcuffs."

Drago

After Four Years of Wedded Bliss

Aimee and I attended services at Etim Cathedral at least once a month. The grandeur of the cathedral never failed to impress, its towering spires and stained-glass windows reflecting centuries of devotion. The other times we fellowshipped with Topaz and Shae. Over the past year, Shae had taken it upon himself to form a Bible study group, inspired by Sapphire's husband's best friend, Regan Wellington.

Glancing around the cathedral, I couldn't recall ever seeing it as packed as it was today. The pews overflowed with people, some even standing outside, craning their necks for a glimpse inside. All of this, for what should have been a simple christening.

The archbishop's voice echoed through the hallowed space, filled with reverence and warmth. "It's a good thing when parents bring their children to the house of the Lord to be blessed. Can the parents, Aimee and Drago Baas, come forward? And would *all* the godparents please join us?"

I couldn't help but smile at the mention of godparents. We hadn't just chosen the obvious—Topaz and Shae, but also Kara, who had become fast friends with Topaz and Aimee after marrying Philippe Burgio. Philippe rose to accompany his wife.

Crown Prince Jordan, Jaden, and even Bishop self-appointed themselves as godparents. Our baby's godparents could be a poster of diversity for the United Nations. The thought made the corners of my lips turned up with a smile. As the ten of us made our way to the front—ten, because the self-appointed godparents also included Leila and Tanisha— the murmur of the crowd grew louder. I could feel the weight of over two thousand eyes on us, watching one of the most public, high-profile baby christenings the cathedral had seen for a while. There were others, but not public. I resolved that next time I'd take a page from my friends' book and do something way more private.

Standing in the center, I glanced at Aimee, who held our daughter close, her tiny body wrapped securely in a soft, white blanket. Aimee's face glowed with a quiet strength, her love for our child radiating in every gesture, every glance. Our daughter, snug in her mother's arms, let out a soft coo, her eyes half-closed as if the peace of the moment lulled her to close her eyes.

The archbishop stepped forward, his robes sweeping the floor as he gently took our daughter into his arms. We all gathered around him—our extended family, a group of people I had come to cherish deeply, even Jordan.

"May you, as parents, raise this child in the way of the Lord," the archbishop said, his voice steady and full of authority. "So that when she is older, she will not depart from it. Godparents, you are many, if I may say so." Laughter and chuckles came from the congregation. He continued, "You are charged with helping this child to grow spiritually, to be a guiding light in her life."

Aimee leaned into me, her warmth a steady presence at my side. Her eyes glistened, releasing a few tears as she blinked. My own emotions stirred deep within, the moment bringing a sting to my eyes that I quickly blinked away. The weight of the archbishop's words settled over me.

The archbishop held up our daughter as he spoke, his voice ringing out clear and strong. "We welcome Abigail Dorte Minerva Baas into the Christian family, a member of the body of Christ."

When Aimee suggested Minerva as one of the middle names for our daughter, the gesture touched me. With Aimee and Abigail, God gave me a double blessing, which I certainly didn't expect.

The archbishop continued, "May Abigail Dorte Minerva Baas live a life filled with God's grace, peace, and love. And all say Amen."

The word "Amen" rolled through the cathedral like a wave, voices rising in unison, filling the vast space with a powerful sense of community. I leaned down, pressing a kiss to Aimee's head. I stepped forward to take our daughter from the archbishop, her tiny form fitting perfectly in my arms. The cathedral erupted in cheers, the sound bouncing off the high ceilings and echoing through the ancient stone walls. This moment, this celebration of life and faith, would no doubt feature front and center in the social pages of the *Etim Chronicle*.

Our entourage—no, our family—returned to their seats. Aimee and I settled back with our daughter cradled in my arms, wearing booties that her mother made. They were hideous... but yet beautiful because they were made with love.

If you love my books and want to learn more about Bishop, click below to join my newsletter and download Bishop's Date, a free prequel to his story.

https://dl.bookfunnel.com/2mn9x56lhm

Blurb

I wasn't looking for love.

My focus was on expanding my company. Was it because I didn't believe in love?

Nope.

I'd already had my happily ever after, and I was totally fine with that.

But then came a persistent woman, and an unexpected dilemma that could be solved with a barter agreement. She wasn't my fake girlfriend—because I'm too old for all that pretending crap—but she was my plus one.

The last thing I thought I wanted turned out to be the one thing I really needed.

And someone is willing to go to any length to make sure I don't get another happily ever after.

Drago's Touch is a riveting story featuring a wealthy protector with elements of suspense as the heroine confronts past trauma. It unfolds a second chance at love in this billionaire romance, weaving together inspirational themes with dual POVs. Expect a journey filled with twists, turns, and surprises, all spiced up with the signature flair of N. R. Emerald.

Printed in Dunstable, United Kingdom

77923732R00167